CW00797411

THE UNINVITED

ANN EVANS

The Uninvited

Cover image original image by Enrique Meseguer at Pixabay
with additional creative changes by Rob Tysall. Back cover
image and design by Rob Tysall.

The Uninvited was first published by Astraea Press in 2014.
This edition published by Words & Images UK

ISBN: 9798550387696

For my family and friends. Thank you for the support you always show. And a special dedication to my old friends from the days of working at the Coventry Telegraph, where the idea for this story was sparked.

The Uninvited

There's something sinister in the attic. It creeps in when no one is looking. Everyone says the noises Katie can hear is bats, but then everyone seems to be lying, hiding some dark secret. And why has the attic door been bricked up?

Everything has changed for the worse Katie realises when she's forced to stay with her granddad and cousin Vanessa at the old bakehouse. He is just a frightened shadow of himself while Vanessa, who used to be such fun, is spiteful and unpleasant. She even looks different – Gothic and macabre.

And there's rumours of vampires. Katie once loved the spooky stories her cousin would tell, but now Vanessa's stories have a sinister touch as she prepares a surprise party for herself. Puzzled how someone can hold a surprise party for themselves, Katie is told, "Wait and see what the surprise is..."

Chapter One

Now that it was twilight he returned, skittering up the side wall of the old bakehouse, finding footholds in the brickwork, finger-holds amongst the creeping ivy. Effortless and silent, he scaled the sheer wall towards the wooden doorway at the top of the house, beneath the eaves.

If anyone had been watching, they couldn't have said whether the figure was human or monstrosity, simply a large dark shadow moving like a large crawling reptile up the wall.

The old doorway beneath the eaves had once been used to lower sacks of flour down to the ground for the village baker to make bread. Now it had no use except to allow him access to the house.

He tugged the splintering timber and the door creaked open. As lithe as a serpent, he slithered inside.

The musty odour of flour still lingered. Traces lay between the cracks in the attic floorboards. In the shadowy corner, a pile of empty flour sacks hung discarded over the rafters. And the big grinding wheel, once the heart of the old bakehouse, had long since ceased its beating.

As he eased the door back into place, blackness engulfed the oppressive room, and tiny particles of stale flour swarmed briefly into the air before settling again. He took longer to settle, although his footsteps were soft against the old timber floorboards.

The wooden doorway set amongst the old brickwork had warped through time, and now shafts of moonlight glinted through the splintered fragments of wood, bathing a corner of the room in pale silver light.

He stretched out his hand, piercing a silvery shaft and grasped the heavy, dark fabric that lay crumpled on the floor. It made a soft swishing sound as he threw it around his shoulders, swathing him in black, merging him once more into the shadows. Then sinking down onto his knees, he crawled silently into the darkest recess of the attic, where he settled down – to wait.

****

Your grandfather is a good man – a kind man…deep down.

Katie's mother's words echoed in her mind as the taxi left the tiny railway station just outside Witchaven Village and threaded its way towards the old bakehouse. Well, he hadn't been kind enough to meet her off the train, nor had Vanessa, which was odd.

Even though Katie, at fourteen and a half, was eighteen months younger than her cousin, they had always been the best of friends. It was strange that she hadn't been at the station if Granddad had been too busy to meet her.

"Oh well," Katie sighed as she neared the isolated

7

bakehouse. Vanessa was probably out with friends and Granddad was probably at some meeting or other. He was always involved in committees. He liked organising, giving orders, shouting, bossing people around.

He's a good man…

Katie felt suddenly homesick. She hated leaving her mum in the hospital, but with her being so ill, Granddad was the only relative to care for her.

Her cousin Vanessa had lived with Granddad and Nanna since she was a toddler. Her parents had been killed in a car crash, so they'd brought her up. But now Nanna was dead too, from a sudden heart attack at Christmas.

Katie thought back to her last visit here, seven months ago – the funeral. It had been the saddest, most awful visit here to Witchaven ever. Vanessa had been broken-hearted. Granddad had been his usual self though, stiff upper lip, not shedding a tear.

Poor Vanessa, Katie thought as the taxi pulled up outside their home. Stuck with bossy old Granddad. She paid her fare and clambered out.

He was an ex-sergeant major, big and loud with a voice that made your ears ring. He was always telling people what to do, ordering them about. She and Vanessa used to giggle at the way his white handlebar moustache would twitch when he barked out his orders. Sometimes, though, he would get so high and mighty that the only one who dared answer back was Nanna.

For as long as Katie could remember, he had been involved in village life. Her mum described him as a pillar of society. Katie guessed he liked bossing committees about too.

She stood for a moment as the taxi drove away. The house was almost shrouded by the oak, elm, and chestnut trees of Oatmeal Woods. On holidays in the past, she and Vanessa would go exploring in the woods, which was fun, even if her cousin did enjoy scaring her with spooky stories about the mystical characters that lived deep in the woodland.

Katie's gaze switched to the imposing building. It was centuries old with its huge mill wheel smothered in creeping ivy. Her eyes were drawn to the doorway at the top of the house – the miller's doorway where sacks of grain would, long ago, be hauled up for grinding. She and Vanessa often played in the attic. Katie's mum used to worry they would accidentally fall through the doorway. But they always had such fun up there, even if they did end up dusty with old flour.

Looking forward to seeing Vanessa again, Katie rattled the heavy brass door knocker, hoping her cousin would be home.

Granddad was so overbearing and loud, he made her nervous.

But she was beginning to think no one was home,

as it was minutes before the door finally creaked slowly open. Smoky the cat emerged first and wrapped itself around Katie's ankles. And then Granddad appeared.

"Granddad?" Katie uttered, startled by his appearance. He seemed smaller than she remembered. The same thick white hair, the same white handlebar moustache, but his shoulders were hunched and there was a look in his eyes that startled her. A haunted look.

He stared at her for some moments, his pale eyes blank as if his thoughts were far, far away. Finally, he exclaimed, "Katie! I'd forgotten. Come in, come in."

He drew back his shoulders and studied her like a sergeant inspecting his troops. This was more like it, Katie thought, more like his usual self.

"You've grown!" he said. "Still skinny though. How's your mother?"

"She…she was quite poorly when I left the hospital," Katie answered, then afraid she might start crying – which he would never stand for, she quickly changed the subject. "How are you, Granddad?"

"Me? Never better. And you're not to worry about your mother. She's a strong woman. Now come along, I'll get you something to eat. I imagine you're just like your cousin, eat like a horse and never put on an ounce."

Katie frowned. "I don't remember Vanessa having a big appetite."

A muscle twitched in his cheek. "Since…since your

nan passed away, probably her way of compensating."

His shoulders slumped again, and he shuffled rather than marched down the cool, tiled hallway into the kitchen. Katie thought how old and weary he looked.

He cut her a chunk of quiche and sliced up a tomato. "There you go! Can't have you starving. I'll make us a pot of tea."

"Thank you," Katie said, trying to smile. He was making an effort to appear as his old self, but it was an effort. She had already glimpsed the old man he'd become. A stooped old man with a haunted, faraway look in his eyes. No longer a man to be feared – more a man to be pitied.

"Where's Vanessa, Granddad? I can't wait to see her again."

A teacup slipped from his hands and smashed on the red tiled floor. As he stooped to clear away the broken china, Katie saw the expression on his face – that same strange, haunted look.

"Let me help you," Katie offered, but he dismissed her offer with a flap of his hand.

"I can manage, eat your supper. Your cousin's probably upstairs in her room."

Katie sank back into her chair, feeling confused, lost and lonely. She was missing home, missing her mum. She wished Vanessa would come down. There wouldn't be this awful atmosphere if Vanessa was around.

Vanessa was fun; she could always make her laugh – or shiver. Vanessa was the best storyteller ever, and there was nothing Katie liked better than curling up under the duvet while Vanessa told her some dark and mysterious tale of witches and goblins.

She tried to eat, but the food felt dry in her mouth. It was strange too without Nanna pottering around. In fact, everything was strange.

The silence between her and her granddad went on and on. Finally, in an attempt to lighten the mood, she ventured, "Are you still involved with your committees, Granddad?"

"Oh yes, most certainly," he answered, brightening instantly. "I'm Chairman of the Parish Council and on the Board of School Governors. Oh yes, and a magistrate now too."

As he spoke, his expression became animated, no longer a cowering old man. His back straightened, and even his moustache seemed to bristle.

"Wow! How do you get time for all that?" Katie asked, preferring him in this mood. She didn't know that stooped old man at all.

"I never idle my time away. Life's too precious to…" His voice trailed away, and he struggled to finish what he was saying, "to waste."

He had to be thinking about Nanna. He probably missed her more than he would admit. Katie wondered if she should give him a hug, but she didn't dare, so she remained seated and said softly, "Nanna had a happy life…"

"Nanna?" He frowned, as if he hadn't a clue what she was talking about. Then, "Ah yes, your nan, fine woman. Well, I must get on. Twilight meeting at the Town Hall. We're getting close to the election of the mayor."

Katie lowered her eyes. No, he hadn't changed. His committee work was still the most important thing in his life. She must have imagined that haunted look.

She forced herself to appear cheerful. "So, who's going to be elected mayor? I can't imagine anyone more suitable than you."

His pale eyes suddenly sparkled. "Well, between you and me, I've heard I'm in the running."

"That's good," Katie replied, pleased to see his craggy face break into a real smile. But just as swiftly, it vanished. The sparkle died in his eyes and in slunk that stooped, haunted look again.

Only this time he seemed to shrink before her eyes, curling up, like a beaten dog cowering before its master.

"Granddad!" Katie cried, jumping to her feet. "What's wrong?"

Then a prickling sensation at the nape of her neck warned her that they were no longer alone. She spun around.

Standing in the doorway, was Vanessa.

She was dressed in black. Black from head to toe. A long floating black skirt that reached her ankles and a fine black shirt that hung loosely from her thin shoulders with a silky black vest beneath it. Her raven hair had grown longer; she wore it loose, framing a face that was almost pure white – except for her blood-red lipstick. There was no hint of her overeating to compensate for losing her nan. She was tall and willowy and beautiful.

Although the dramatic Gothic appearance of her cousin surprised Katie, she ran and threw her arms around her. "Vanessa, it's brilliant to see you again!"

But Vanessa stood rigid, arms at her sides, expressionless, projecting an aura of cold, stark bleakness that left Katie feeling uncomfortable and unwelcome.

"You're here then," said Vanessa, her voice flat, emotionless, as Katie stepped awkwardly away from her cousin. "Didn't Granddad tell you? This isn't a good time."

The unfriendly welcome shocked Katie. "But, there's nowhere else, no one else…" She looked to her granddad for support.

The old man mumbled inaudibly, lowering his head, avoiding Katie's gaze. Confused, she looked back at her cousin.

Vanessa's darkly rimmed eyes were hostile. "Well, just don't expect things to be like they were. Nothing's the way it was." She glared at the old man. "Is it, Granddad?"

Without a word he shuffled towards the sink, shoulders slumped, head bent, a pathetic shadow of himself. Vanessa flicked back her hair, looking triumphant.

Katie stared at them both, shocked by how things had changed. Their roles had been reversed. Vanessa was the domineering one now while Granddad seemed totally under her power.

What on earth had happened here?

Chapter Two

The old bakehouse was a catacomb of rooms and passageways. When they were younger, Katie and Vanessa had played for hours, running and hiding in all the alcoves and bedrooms.

Now Katie had been given a room at the back of the house. A room full of shadows, with one tiny window that overlooked the battered roofs of the outbuildings and sheds. Had Vanessa forgotten that this was the one room she disliked when they were younger?

Or was that why she'd put her here?

Granddad went out to his meeting and Katie was left to do her unpacking alone. She couldn't have felt more unwelcome if they'd slammed the door in her face.

With a sigh, she began to hang her clothes in the wardrobe. It was a huge, ornately carved piece of furniture made from dark red mahogany with a long, thin mirror in the door. The furniture in this particular room was one of the reasons she disliked it so much. She could see faces in the wood carvings, ugly faces of monsters and demons, snarling and leering. As she unpacked, she tried not to think about them.

Once her clothes were hung tidily, she clicked the wardrobe door shut and started unpacking her smaller case. The sound of something creaking made her spin around.

She gasped as her own startled reflection swept past in the wardrobe door mirror. Immediately she realised she couldn't have shut the door properly and groaned for being so jumpy. She closed it again and got back to placing her personal things, including a framed photo of her mum, on the dressing table.

The dresser was carved from the same dark red mahogany as the wardrobe. It had a large mirror in the centre and two movable side mirrors that reflected her face from every angle. Through one of the side mirrors, she caught sight of something moving again and she spun around, heart thumping. The wardrobe door was swinging open yet again.

For a second Katie hesitated, watching it sway on its old brass hinges, while the hideous faces in the carvings snarled at her.

Hating the wardrobe, hating this room, she found a piece of cardboard and wedged the door firmly shut.

After unpacking, she went downstairs. The house was deserted except for the cat. It ran meowing to the door to be let out. Katie opened it, and with a glance behind her at the deserted kitchen, she followed Smoky outside.

The sun was setting, casting brilliant red streaks across the skyline, turning trees into dark silhouettes. Birds by the hundred were returning to roost for the night.

Katie wandered down the overgrown path; the

garden had become unruly, a wilderness almost. Nanna had loved gardening but now that she was gone, the garden had been left to grow wild. In a chaotic way it was still lovely – a profusion of trees and rhododendron bushes edged both sides of the uncut lawns. And rambling wild roses and honeysuckle tangled over the roofs of the old wooden sheds and barns.

At the bottom of the garden, a wooden fence separated the house from the farmer's fields and open countryside. It was comforting to see the herd of golden coloured Jersey cows still there, as always.

It was almost dark now, and bats were starting to dip and dive through the swarms of midges. As Smoky went off on the prowl, Katie wandered down to look at the cattle as they settled down for the night. Some were already lying down; others were standing, tails swishing, mouths chewing.

Then something which brought back happy memories caught Katie's eye: the old swing was still there, slightly rusty, but in working order. It was just two chunky lengths of rope slotted through a short plank of wood hanging from a sturdy branch of an elm tree. Unable to resist, Katie seated herself on the wooden seat and gently swung back and forth.

The seat had been worn smooth over the years, and happy times flooded back of when she and Vanessa had squeezed on it together as they discussed important issues of the world—the places they would visit when they were older, and all the things they would see and do. And of course, the times when Vanessa would send shivers down her spine with creepy tales of ghosts and vampires.

Katie swung to and fro, her re-living happier times here, when Nanna was alive and her mum wasn't sick, and Vanessa was fun.

She had no idea how long she'd sat with her thoughts drifting, but then she heard crunching footsteps of someone marching down the lane. Jumping off the swing, she ran back up the garden and stood by the mill wheel where she could see the lane through gaps in the bushes.

It was Granddad returning from his meeting. He marched smartly along the lane, arms swinging, like the ex-military man that he was. But as he neared home, his step faltered, his shoulders slouched, and his arms hung limply. By the time he'd reached the house his whole demeanor seemed to have shriveled up.

Katie felt utterly sad – for everyone.

She went into the house through the back door and met him in the hall, forcing herself to sound cheerful. "Hi, Granddad, did you have a good meeting?"

He brightened the moment he saw her. "Yes, satisfactory. Things are looking good regarding the mayor business…"

His voice faltered as he glanced up the stairs. Katie looked too and saw Vanessa standing like some Gothic queen on the top landing. There must have been a window open because her long black skirt and black hair fluttered in a breeze from somewhere.

Flustered, Granddad hurried into his downstairs study. "I...I have some paperwork to do. I'll see you in the morning. Good night."

"Good night."

The door clicked shut and Katie heard the key turning in the lock as Vanessa swept past her on her way to the kitchen. Katie followed her.

Without speaking, Vanessa went to the fridge and began piling food onto a plate. Katie watching her for a while then said: "Why did you say it wasn't a good time for me to be here?"

Vanessa simply glanced coldly at her. Her icy blue eyes were highlighted by black liner and mascara. It made a striking contrast against her white foundation. All made up for a Gothic disco or something, Katie thought.

"Well?" demanded Katie, folding her arms.

Vanessa looked away. Dismissively she answered, "Because I'm busy."

"Doing what?" Katie insisted, refusing to be dismissed offhandedly by a cousin who was acting so peculiarly. Vanessa might frighten Granddad for some unknown reason, but she certainly didn't frighten her.

"I'm arranging my surprise party if you must know."

"Your sixteenth? Your birthday is this Saturday, isn't it?" said Katie, then frowning added: "Hang on, how can you arrange a surprise party for yourself?"

Vanessa cast her a sideways glance and her blood-red lips curved into a cold, calculating smile. "Wait and see what the surprise is."

A shiver ran down Katie's spine and she stared at her cousin, a strange, unnerving feeling churning in the pit of her stomach.

Somehow, she knew that whatever the surprise was, it wasn't going to be a pleasant one.

****

A bedside lamp would have been a nice touch, Katie thought as she was plunged into pitch blackness when she turned off her bedroom light. To compensate, she opened her curtains, allowing the moonlight in. She lay cocooned in the duvet, watching the grey clouds drifting slowly past her window, occasionally allowing the light from some distant star to glimmer through.

The heavy bedroom furniture cast long shadows around the room, and every time she moved, it registered in the dressing table mirrors, making her think there was someone else in the room with her. The sensation quickened her heartbeat every time.

As her eyes became accustomed to the gloom, she could make out the patterns of the ornate carvings in the wardrobe and dresser. Swirls and crests became snarling demonic faces. Knots in the wood became eyes, watching her. And to make matters worse, there were noises, creaking noises above her.

Noises in the attic.

At first, she guessed it was just the old wooden beams settling for the night, or air locked in the plumbing. But as she lay there in the silence of the night, the noises took on a pattern.

The creaking sounds moved from one side of the attic to the other, like someone pacing around up there.

It had to be Vanessa or Granddad. But she hadn't heard either of them go past her bedroom door, which was the only way up to the attic: along the passageway, around the corner, up the little stairs, through the door, and into the attic. Katie knew it like the back of her hand.

The creaking continued, and as she lay staring up at the ceiling, her eyes followed the sounds. Back and forth, back and forth.

And then they stopped, directly above her head. Katie lay deathly still, her eyes huge, scarcely breathing. An icy cold prickling sensation crawling over her skin.

Someone was in the attic. Someone —or something.

****

In the dead of night he slithered out from his resting

22

place. He moved softly – as silent as the grave, disturbing no one.

He selected his victim with care. Those that were deep in sleep, and oblivious to the malevolent presence so close by. Under the moonlight his sharp teeth glinted, so needle sharp that his victim felt nothing as incisors sank into their flesh and he drank their thick, warm blood.

****

Katie didn't recall closing her eyes, but she must have, eventually, because she awoke to find the sun shining into her face. She got up and dressed, still spooked by the feeling that someone had been watching her last night from up in the attic.

She felt stiff from the uncomfortable bed and she rubbed the back of her neck and stretched her shoulders.

Vanessa and Granddad were eating breakfast in silence downstairs. Scrambled eggs and bacon were keeping warm in the oven for her. Katie doubted that it was Vanessa's gesture, and she thanked her granddad as she sat down at the table.

The chinking of cutlery against china and the soft sounds of chewing made for an oppressive silence around the table. It was so unlike the lively mealtimes she and her mum shared and so different from how it used to be. In the past she and Vanessa would be chattering away so much that Granddad would bark, "Less chat, more chew!" Their Nanna would look at them both and chuckle.

Katie absolutely hated this unfriendly atmosphere and to break the oppressive silence she told them about the noises coming from the attic.

"Noises?" Vanessa repeated. "What sort of noises?"

"Creaking noises," Katie replied. "I thought it was you or Granddad up there, except it sounded like someone tiptoeing about. It was a bit creepy actually."

Granddad suddenly began to cough violently.

Alarmed, Katie jumped up and patted his back in case he was choking. Eventually he calmed down, but a trickle of sweat rolled down his reddened cheek.

"Are you all right?" Katie asked anxiously. "Have a sip of your tea."

Vanessa hadn't moved an inch. She'd sat, quite unconcerned that their granddad had almost choked. Katie glared at her.

He mopped his forehead. "Piece of toast went down the wrong way, I'm all right. Don't panic." Nevertheless, he took a pill from a little box in his cardigan pocket and slipped it under his tongue.

Katie frowned. "What's that for?"

"It's for my angina."

"Angina… your heart?" Katie gasped, horrified.

"It's nothing," he assured her. "Nothing to worry

about."

"So long as he keeps taking the pills," Vanessa butted in callously.

Sadly, Katie realised how nasty her cousin had become. No wonder Granddad didn't boss her around anymore.

When everything was calm again Vanessa said pointedly, "Well, what about those noises, Granddad? Any ideas?"

"No," he murmured, his eyelids fluttering. "No, I've no idea."

Katie glanced at him. He was sweating again.

"Actually," Vanessa continued, placing her knife and fork precisely down. "I often hear noises coming from the attic. It's like someone moving around, moving blindly, in the dark, feeling for some way out...." Her voice became a whisper. Slowly and melodramatically she murmured, "Backward and forwards, arms outstretched, feeling their way in the darkness. But there is no way out. Is there, Granddad?"

The old man gulped his tea, almost choking again. His eyes were downturned, not looking at anyone.

"No way out at all," Vanessa continued, as if driving home a point. And then, turning her pale, wide eyes innocently towards Katie, she said in a totally casual manner, "Actually it's bats. We've got bats in the attic. I admit they can sound a bit odd at times."

"Bats?" Katie gasped. "We've never had bats in the

attic! Anyway, it couldn't have been bats, it was like footsteps – heavy footsteps, trying to be quiet."

"It's bats, I'm telling you, nothing to hurt anyone," Vanessa stressed. Then her tone of voice changed again, becoming hard, spitting the words like venom at her granddad. "I mean, it's not as if we have a ghost or a skeleton in the attic – is it, Granddad?"

The old man started to choke again.

Chapter Three

Katie did her best to finish breakfast, but the atmosphere was depressing. At the first opportunity she got up from the table. "Could I use your phone please, Granddad? I want to call the hospital to see how Mum is."

"It doesn't work," Vanessa answered for him.

Katie stared at her cousin, wondering if she was lying. Then her granddad said, "There's a fault on the line…"

"They're coming Monday to fix it," Vanessa said.

"Oh, I'll take a walk down to the village then. I wanted to take some flowers to Nanna's grave anyway."

To her surprise Granddad touched her hand. "Your mother will be all right. She's a strong woman. Try not to worry too much."

Katie blinked back sudden tears. Her mum hadn't looked strong when she'd left her in the hospital. She'd looked pale and exhausted.

Katie got out of the house quickly before the tears started to fall. She was halfway down the lane before she realized the sunshine had vanished and a mass of black storm clouds had appeared from nowhere. Way off in the distance she heard the distinct rumble of thunder. Determined, she zipped up her jacket and quickened her step.

It was a ten-minute walk to the village with the lane curling along the outskirts of Oatmeal Woods. When things were different, Vanessa would make up scary stories about the woods' inhabitants. Like the demon woodcutter who would cut your legs off if you should bump into him. And the hobgoblin that lived under the ninth oak who could turn people into toads. And the wicked tooth fairy who lived by the meadow. If you should fall asleep amongst the wildflowers, she would pull out all your teeth while you slept.

As she walked, Katie found herself smiling, remembering the tales she would tell. Whatever could have happened to change things so drastically? They used to be such good friends.

The village was just as she remembered it, and she headed towards the pay phone by the post office and called the hospital. They said her mother had a comfortable night, but no, she couldn't speak to her at the moment as the specialist was with her.

Feeling homesick, Katie wandered around the quaint little craft shops. She bought a miniature china doll for her mother's collection, and a small bunch of freesias for her nanna's grave.

The cemetery was on the outskirts of the village right next to the old parish church of Saint Michael. It was a sprawling cemetery for such a small village, probably because Witchaven had such a long history and some of the graves were centuries old.

She'd never walked there alone before, and twice she had to stop and ask directions. By the time she'd reached the cemetery gates, the sky had turned so black that passing cars had switched their headlights on.

On the day of her nanna's funeral, the wind and rain had sleeted down, disorientating her. Now Katie couldn't recall where exactly the grave was. She wandered around the cemetery, trying to remember.

Like before, big spots of rain began to fall from the thunderous clouds, making Katie realise that this probably wasn't the best place to be in a storm. Still, she'd come this far…

Pulling up her jacket hood, she hurried along the footpaths between the endless rows of gravestones.

There was no one else about—obviously other people had more sense than to go wandering through a cemetery on days like this. It was beginning to feel quite creepy. Vanessa loved it here. So often, her stories were woven around this place.

Keeping to the pathways between crumbling old grey headstones with worn away inscriptions, Katie quickened her step to hurry past the oldest, most ancient crypt in the cemetery. It was the size of a garden shed but made from grey stone blocks. Legend had it that a boy from the seventeenth century was deliberately entombed alive by the villagers. Of course, it could just have been one of Vanessa's stories.

Hurrying by, she glanced at the large stone figure

standing guard over the crypt. She had seen it before, but now, perhaps because of those bats in the attic, the statue took on a new and grotesque image, and Katie felt as if an icy hand had crawled up her spine.

Originally the statue had probably been of an angel. But over time, or perhaps because of vandalism, the head had gone, leaving only these big wings.

It didn't look like an angel anymore.

To Katie, it looked like a bat…a giant bat.

As she hurried past, something else caught her eye. The door of the crypt was open.

She scurried along, glancing back over her shoulder, wishing the area wasn't so deserted. She finally found her nanna's grave just as big splashes of rain dashed down.

She was pleased to see it was well cared for. There was a vase brimming with fresh flowers, and the new headstone was clean and polished. Katie added her freesias and stood for a while with her head bowed in the rain, remembering how lovely her nanna was.

Suddenly the heavens opened. A streak of lightning flashed across the black sky, a deluge of rain dropped from the clouds, and a deafening boom of thunder exploded overhead.

Apologising under her breath to her nanna for not staying longer, but certain she would understand, Katie looked frantically around for some sort of cover.

It wasn't safe to shelter under a tree during a storm,

and the only other place she could see to take shelter was the crypt. Her heart sank.

But there really wasn't any other choice. Reluctantly, she dipped just inside its open doorway, just under cover enough so that the worst of the rain missed her.

She huddled there, watching the torrent of rain lashing down. It quickly formed pools on the pathways, turning white stone to shiny grey…and then she became aware of the coldness.

It wasn't just the weather. A cold clamminess was seeping through her clothing, clinging to her skin. Coldness that was coming from within the crypt.

Warily she glanced over her shoulder into the blackened space. To her horror, although it came as no surprise, she could make out the shape of an oblong tomb.

Where they buried him alive.

A second later there was a sound—a shuffle. Without warning a face appeared directly in front of her out of the gloom.

Shrieking in terror, Katie shot out into the storm, slithering and sliding in the mud and puddles as she fled panic-stricken along the footpath.

But above the noise of the rain and the thunder, she heard someone calling after her.

"Hey! I'm sorry. I didn't mean to freak you out!"

She slowed and glanced back, her heart thudding

wildly. There was a boy standing in the crypt doorway, waving to her. He was wearing a black sweatshirt and black jeans, which may have been the reason for not spotting him right away in the gloom.

"You idiot!" Katie yelled, furious now rather than afraid. He was just a boy, a year or two older than her, she guessed, not a ghost or a skeleton.

"I'm sorry. I didn't mean to scare you," he called, ducking back under cover.

"Well! What on earth were you doing in there anyway?" Katie yelled as rainwater dripped from her nose.

"Same as you, taking shelter from the rain. Come on back, you're getting soaked. It's okay, honest, I don't bite." He grinned, and even from this distance Katie saw what a cute smile he had.

Another crack of lightning directly overhead and a downpour of cold stinging rain helped her decide, and she splashed back through the puddles to the crypt.

"It's colder in here than outside," she complained, standing just under cover.

"Ah! That's probably because of what happened here all those years ago," he said, offering her a tissue to dry her face.

"Thank you…You don't actually believe that old legend, do you? You're as bad as my cousin."

"Nah! It's probably all rubbish. I'm Christian by the way, Christian King. Who are you?"

"I'm the girl you almost scared to death." Katie glared. "You could have warned me you were there."

"I didn't see you. I just turned 'round and there you were. You scared me as much as I scared you!"

"I don't think so!" Katie said, studying him in the murky darkness of the crypt. "What were you doing in the cemetery anyway?"

"I could ask you the same question." His smile took the sting from his words.

"I was putting flowers on my nanna's grave," Katie answered, feeling slightly indignant at having to explain anything to someone who'd just scared the life out of her.

"Well, I don't have any relatives buried here. I was just looking at the bat statue outside. It's always intrigued me. I've got this thing about bats."

"You wouldn't think bats were so wonderful if they were stomping around in your attic at night!"

His eyes lit up. "You've got bats in your attic? How many? What type?"

Katie stared at him like he was mad. "I've absolutely no idea, and besides, that's not a statue of a bat outside. It's an angel without a head."

"Yeah, maybe." He shrugged, moving a bit deeper into the crypt. "The lid on the tomb is falling apart too. Look, you can actually see inside it."

"What? You can see the bones and everything?" Katie exclaimed, pulling a face.

"I guess so, I haven't looked yet. I was just about to. Come on. . ."

Katie had to admit she was curious. Perhaps there was something of Vanessa in her after all. Warily, she followed him.

The clammy coldness of the small shadowy room seeped through her clothing, chilling her to the bone. There wasn't a hint of warmth in here. It was as if the heat from the sun had never penetrated these thick stone walls.

Shivering, she stared at the plain granite tomb. It had no ornamentation, no carvings, just bare stone with another slab as its lid. It looked like it had been thrown on hurriedly, because it was askew leaving a gaping hole at one corner.

Standing together beside the tomb, they both read the worn inscription etched roughly into the stonework:

William Knight
1650 — 1666
May God forgive

"He was just a boy," Katie murmured, trying to recall the tale Vanessa used to tell her.

"Legend says that William Knight was a vampire," said Christian, speaking in a hushed voice, almost like he was scared of speaking too loudly in case it awoke the sleeping vampire. "He was entombed alive because he wouldn't die."

Katie found herself smiling. He reminded her of Vanessa at her storytelling best. She raised her eyebrows at him. "And you believe that, do you?"

"I read it in a local folklore book," he told her enthusiastically. "In the mid-1600s a young stranger was supposed to have moved into the village, and it wasn't long before people found bite marks on their necks. They believed the stranger was drinking their blood as they slept. He was put on trial, found guilty, and sentenced to death."

"And…" interrupted Katie, remembering what Vanessa used to tell her. "They tried hanging him but the branch of the tree snapped. They tried burning him at the stake but a freak rainstorm came from nowhere dousing the flames. So they bundled him into a stone tomb, built a crypt around him, and left him to die."

"That's right," Christian said, the whites of his eyes luminous in the gloom as he stared at her. "How do you know all that?"

Katie laughed. "My cousin reads the same fairytale books as you."

"So you don't think there's any truth in the legend, then?" he mused, feeling around the walls of the crypt. "If you look carefully, there's some drawings scratched on these bricks, sort of bat shapes and hovering creatures, and of course, there's that big bat-angel thing outside."

"It's all nonsense," Katie dismissed, rubbing at her arms.

"But what if it wasn't?" he suggested, his eyes widening. "Can you imagine – this boy, this young vampire, was indestructible. He could live forever."

Katie pulled a face. "On a diet of warm blood! Yuck!"

"And vampires can fly," he breathed. "Just imagine soaring from the rooftops, being able to scale walls. He'd have all the skills and abilities of a bat and the intelligence of man, combined. Just think of the power!"

Katie stared at him, wondering if he could be serious, or if like Vanessa, his imagination just ran away with him. She glanced at the crypt door. "So why do you think the door was open? Gone out for a bite to eat, perhaps?"

"Who knows?" He shrugged, her joke passing over his head. "Anyway, I'm gonna have a look into the tomb. See what I can see."

Katie backed off. "Don't let me stop you!'"

"Chicken!" he said with a grin as he peered down through the gap where the lid was askew.

Katie held her breath, half expecting a skeleton's hand to shoot up and grab him by the throat.

There was an odd look on his face as he stepped back. "Can't see anything."

"And you'd want to?" she gasped, deciding she'd definitely had enough of decrepit old tombs. Rain or no rain, she was getting out of here. To her relief when she stepped outside, the worst of the storm had passed and the rain was easing off. The sky was still grey and cloudy though.

He followed her out, hunching up his shoulders as he caught up with her. "You'd think there'd be bones or rags or something. But there's nothing!"

"There probably never was," Katie dismissed, eager to get away from depressing gravestones. She picked her way around the puddles and headed towards the cemetery gates. It was nice to have someone pleasant to talk to, though. "So why are you so interested in bats?"

He loped along beside her, hands in pockets, shoulders hunched, but continually glancing at her, an excitement about him that warmed her to him. "Bats are ace. I've always been fascinated by them."

She guessed he was about fifteen, a few inches taller than her with black hair plastered to his head because of the rain. Laughter bubbled up inside of her.

"What?"

"The rain's made your hair all sleek. You look a bit like a vampire yourself now!"

"I've got fangs too!" he said, pulling a face, so that Katie could see two small pointed incisors. "When I was younger I looked like the kid from the Addams Family."

Katie laughed and realised suddenly that since arriving here, he had been the only person to make her laugh. "I'm Katie by the way. I'm staying with my granddad and cousin at the old bakehouse while my mum's in hospital."

"Really? What's wrong with her?"

Katie took a deep breath and tried to keep her voice steady. "She's...she's got a tumour. They're removing it."

"She'll pull through, you'll see," he said, sounding as if he knew that for certain.

"Yes, I know she will," Katie agreed, wishing she felt as confident as he seemed to.

"Honestly. I have an instinct for these things. Must be my bat-like echolocation. Hey, and you say you've got bats in your attic – you wouldn't let me see them, would you?"

Katie drew up her shoulders. "My cousin says it's bats but I'm not so sure..."

"You haven't looked for yourself, then?"

She shrugged. "No, I haven't."

"We could take a look together," he suggested, raising one dark eyebrow hopefully.

That wasn't such a bad idea. Perhaps if she saw them for herself, those night-time noises might not be quite so eerie. "I suppose you could. Don't see why not."

"Brilliant!"

****

Smoky the cat greeted them when they got back to the house, then shot off into the woods like a streak of lightning when Christian stooped to stroke her.

"What's got into her?" Katie puzzled.

"Cats tend not to like me." he shrugged. "Is it okay if I come in?"

"Yes, of course. The attic is this way."

He followed her his footsteps surprisingly soft on the creaky stairs, and twice she glanced back to see if he was still with her. Each time, she caught him with an intense look on his face, which quickly changed to a smile when he saw her looking at him.

A tingle of unease crept through her. She actually knew nothing about this boy. On impulse she said, "I imagine my granddad will be in his study, and my cousin will be in her room."

She hoped she'd got the message across that she wasn't alone in the house, even though she probably was. She led the way along the passageway past her room. Walking on, she went around the corner and up the little flight of stairs to the attic door. "Almost there…"

She stopped abruptly as she came face to face with a wall. The attic doorway had disappeared.

In disbelief, she touched it. It felt solid. A brick wall, plastered, wallpapered, with a painting of a poppy field hanging where the door should have been.

For a second, she felt dizzy, totally disorientated.

"It's been bricked up!" she finally gasped, utterly confused.

Christian stared at her. "What?"

Katie pushed against the wall, her head spinning. "This is crazy! You can see by the little staircase that there should be a door at the top. Why on earth would they brick it up?"

"Perhaps the attic isn't safe to go into," Christian suggested, looking disappointed.

Katie stared at the wall. Vanessa's words echoing around her head. *It's not as if we have a ghost or a skeleton in the attic, is it Granddad...* "What do you mean, not safe?" Katie accused, rounding on him.

Christian held his hands up in defense. "Hey! I only meant that the floorboards could have rotted or something." He frowned. "What did you think I meant?"

Katie shrugged helplessly. "I don't know."

He pulled a face. "Isn't there another way in?"

"Only through the miller's door in the side of the house," Katie sighed. "Otherwise no, there's no way in."

An odd little thought jumped into her head from nowhere...

And no way out.

Chapter Four

"Granddad, why have you bricked up the attic door?" Katie asked over dinner that evening.

The old man and her cousin immediately stopped eating.

She saw her granddad take a deep breath, as if he'd been dreading the question. Vanessa was watching him from the corner of her eye.

"Because the floor's unsafe," he answered at last. "It's gone rotten. It's too dangerous to go up there."

Katie frowned. "Isn't it a bit drastic to brick up the doorway? The attic always had a bolt and padlock anyway. What if a future owner wants to renovate the place?"

"I don't!" Vanessa cut in, placing her knife and fork down and looking Katie steadily in the eye.

Katie stared back. "*You* don't? Excuse me, but what if Granddad has other plans for this house? He might want to sell up and buy a little cottage somewhere. Mightn't you, Granddad?"

He avoided her eyes. "Er, no, no I don't expect so."

Vanessa looked smug, and Katie had to bite back the question that demanded an answer. But she couldn't ask it in front of her granddad.

After dinner he went to his study and Vanessa turned her icy blue eyes to Katie. "Well, go on then, ask me. I know you're dying to."

Katie thought hard for a moment, and then said, "Nanna told us that when she and Granddad died, this house would be sold by auction and the money divided between all the surviving relatives equally. You and my family, and we've got relatives in Australia, haven't we?" Katie looked at her cousin questioningly. "Since when did it all become yours?"

The older girl's face took on a smug, conceited expression. "Since Granddad changed his will actually."

Katie stared in disbelief. "Why would he do that?"

"How would I know? Maybe he just loves me best. I have lived with him since I was a toddler. I'm like a daughter to him."

"Some daughter! He's scared to death of you!" Katie exclaimed angrily. "When you're near him, he's like a broken, defeated old man."

"You're imagining things."

"I'm not blind, Vanessa. He's scared of you. But why? What have you done to him?"

"I've not *done* anything." Vanessa snapped, turning aside. "He's the one who bossed everyone around and made everyone's lives a misery. Maybe he's realised that he went too far and he's trying to make up for his nastiness."

Katie looked doubtful. "That doesn't explain why you're to inherit everything. Granddad bossed everyone around…unless there's something you're not telling me."

"Such as?"

Katie stared at her cousin, trying to figure it out. It just didn't make sense. If he had made a new will it meant that he'd deliberately cut out all of his family and relatives in favour of someone he was frightened of. Then it became clear as day.

"Of course! You've forced him to change his will, haven't you? He wouldn't have done this by choice. You've made him!"

Vanessa threw her arms wide and laughed. "Oh yes, just look at me. I'm so hugely terrifying, aren't I?"

Looking at her cousin with her macabre clothing and makeup, that long straight black hair and white face, Katie was tempted to say that on a dark night she could very well frighten the life out of someone. She bit back the catty remark and shook her head. "I'm not saying you're a physical threat to Granddad, but there are other ways."

"Maybe I put a gun to his head?"

"Maybe you did," Katie agreed, "in your own way."

Vanessa sneered. "You're being ridiculous. You're just jealous because you've been disinherited. Well, that's just your bad luck." And tossing back her hair she swept out of the kitchen, leaving behind only her heady lingering perfume.

Katie stood there trembling. She hated arguments,

particularly with someone who had once been so close.

What on earth had gone on here? How had Vanessa turned the tables like this? Now she was the one to give the orders and Granddad was the one to jump to them.

Something major had happened – but what?

****

Lost in thought, Katie wandered down the garden and sat on the swing. Granddad was frightened of Vanessa, despite them both denying it. But was Vanessa a physical threat? Or was it something deeper?

Gradually twilight swept away the last threads of daylight, turning the sky inky black, etching the clouds in silver. In the field, the cows settled down for the night, and one by one the bats appeared, swooping through the air catching midges.

Still lost in thought, gently swinging back and forth, Katie thought about her mum. She desperately wished she was better and out of hospital so she could go home. A sudden movement amongst the cattle brought Katie back to earth. A calf jumped to its feet, startled by something. Its alarm instantly transmitting to the rest of the herd, and a moment later they were all on their feet, clearly disturbed by something.

Curious, Katie wandered down towards the fence, wondering if a fox was scaring them or a stray dog maybe, but it was difficult to make out distinct shapes now with nightfall descending so rapidly.

Then she saw what was upsetting them. A bat was flitting about over the cattle, swooping at them — as if attacking them.

That was odd. Bats didn't behave like that normally. And ordinarily cows wouldn't be worried about a bat, but the entire herd seemed really spooked by the solitary creature.

As she watched, Katie saw it land on the ground and to her horror began hopping towards one of the calves. Hopping like some ugly prancing giant insect.

Worse then, it fluttered onto the calf's back and scuttled right up to its neck, seeming to cling on by its teeth while the poor animal ran off in fright, with the bat still attached to its neck.

Katie felt sick.

Bats didn't attack animals. Her skin crawled. This was no normal bat... it was a blood-sucking bat. Sickened, she raced into the house with her hands wrapped around her throat in case one decided to make a meal out of her too.

Before going to bed, she searched her bedroom for any ventilation holes or cracks that might allow a bat to find its way in. Then she secured all the windows and left the light on. Bats didn't go into the light – did they?

The noises in the attic now took on a horrible new meaning. It wasn't just bats up there. It was blood-sucking bats. Vampire bats!

Katie slept badly, imagining there were bats flitting around her hair – bats which, when you got up close, had human faces – Vanessa's face.

She woke early, nevertheless Granddad was already in the kitchen, cooking breakfast. Katie was glad there was no sign of Vanessa.

The second he saw Katie, he turned off the cooker, took her hand, and whispered, "Quickly before she comes down."

With his finger to his lips, he led her into his study. Closing the door behind them, he silently unlocked his writing bureau and took out a small battered suitcase. "For you Katie," he whispered. "For you and your mother."

Totally puzzled she whispered, "What is it?"

He took a tiny key from his pocket and opened the little case. It was crammed full of brown envelopes and packages. He opened one and to Katie's amazement, she saw that it contained her nanna's jewellery. Another packet revealed documents; another was full of letters and photographs.

"Your nan's possessions – your cousin is *not* getting everything." He opened up another package full of money.

Katie gasped. "There must be hundreds of pounds here!"

"Your nan's savings. At least you and your mother will get something. I'm sorry you won't get your fair share of the house."

"I don't care about that, I'm just worried about you," Katie stressed. "I know Vanessa has forced you to change your will, and I know you're afraid of her. But why? What's happened here, Granddad?"

For a moment he looked ready to explain, and then he squared his shoulders, the harsh, brash granddad that she knew, returned. "Nothing happened! And I'm certainly not frightened of the girl. Good gracious! What a silly thing to say. Come along now, breakfast is about ready."

"But..."

"No buts," he said, ushering her into the hall. "Just get that case hidden, no need to tell her."

Someone rapped on the front door then, giving Katie no opportunity to question him further.

It was the postman. He had a large parcel for Vanessa. Katie hid the little suitcase in her wardrobe before going along to Vanessa's room with the parcel.

Her cousin's black-rimmed eyes lit up when she saw the delivery. "At last! I was starting to think it wouldn't arrive in time."

"What is it?"

"Party decorations," answered Vanessa, taking the package into her bedroom and actually smiling as she ripped off the brown paper. Katie hung around hoping her cousin would miraculously return to being the friend she used to be. But Vanessa raised her eyebrows at her. "So, what are you waiting for?"

"Just curious," Katie answered, doing her best to be friendly. "Where's the party going to be? Here, or have you hired a hall?"

"Here," Vanessa replied, slicing through more packaging with her sharp fingernails. "But don't get excited. My party is for invited guests only – and you're not on the list."

"Why are you being so horrible?" Katie cried. "You're horrible to me and you're horrible to Granddad."

"Granddad is the horrible one." Then murmuring quietly under her breath, she added, "It's his fault that Nanna died."

Katie stared at her cousin, horrified. "Why is it his fault? Nanna had a heart attack."

"Yes, and why did she have a heart attack?"

Katie shrugged. "I don't know."

"Because he was ranting and raving, like he always used to," Vanessa spat bitterly. "You should have seen him that day – the day Nanna died. Yelling and shouting, bossing everyone around, upsetting everyone. And all because my boyfriend was up in the attic with me. We weren't up to anything, but would he listen? No, he just went berserk. Nanna tried to calm him, and he pushed her away – he *pushed* her! No wonder she had a heart attack. It's his fault Nanna is dead and he's not going to get away with it!"

"What do you mean?" Katie murmured, shocked to hear that Vanessa blamed her grandfather, although at least that would explain why she was so nasty to him. It didn't explain how she'd managed to turn the tables on him, however.

"Nothing! I don't mean anything," she snapped. Then clamped her lips shut, as if she'd already said too much. After a moment she said, "But I do think you should make other arrangements to be looked after. You don't want to stay here." She looked intensely at Katie. "You really do *not* want to be here."

Her words stung as sharply as the tears that pricked the back of Katie's eyes. Determined that her spiteful cousin wouldn't see her cry, Katie turned and ran downstairs.

She didn't feel like eating, particularly when Vanessa came down for breakfast a few minutes later.

Hurt because of her cousin's unkindness and Granddad's unwillingness to let her help him, Katie decided to give them both something else to think about.

"What sort of bats live around here?" she asked calmly. Vanessa gave a disinterested shrug.

"Pipistrelles, I think," suggested Granddad.

"What do they eat?"

"Insects, I imagine," he mused.

"Not blood, then?" asked Katie innocently. They both stopped eating and stared at her.

"That's vampire bats," said her granddad. "You've nothing to worry about, Katie. They only live in places like South America. Our bats are quite harmless."

"Why?" Vanessa asked curiously.

"I thought I saw a bat attacking a calf last night," she said, shuddering at the memory.

"How big was it?" asked Vanessa.

"About this big," said Katie, indicating its size with her hands. "Bigger than most of the bats I've seen flying around."

Her cousin's eyes gleamed. "Not a full-sized vampire, then?"

"Make fun of me if you like," said Katie. "But I saw a bat jump onto a calf's neck. It spooked the whole herd."

"I'm not making fun," Vanessa said innocently. "I'm asking because there's a rumour going around the village that a black-cloaked figure has been lurking around the woods at night. And apparently he...it...can fly – like a bat."

Katie smiled. "Nice one, Vanessa, I see you haven't lost your touch."

"I'm not making it up. Last Halloween, the old crypt was broken into – you know the one – where that young vampire was entombed alive." Her black-rimmed eyes narrowed and she lowered her voice to a whisper. "Well, it's assumed someone broke in, but of course it could have been someone breaking out...

Anyway, since then people have been reporting sightings of a cloaked figure. Oh well, at least he's only sucking cows' blood, not human's."

Katie shook her head. "I saw a bat attacking a cow, not a human-sized vampire. I think you're losing the plot here, Vanessa."

"I don't think so," said her cousin, leaning across the table, her voice hushed. "Didn't you know, a vampire can change shape? It might appear as human – as normal as you or me, or as a bat. Or as it really is – a life-sized vampire with slick black hair, a black cloak, and long sharp teeth, ready to bite into your throat!"

Katie jumped back as Vanessa's teeth clamped sharply together. "Very funny!" she groaned; nevertheless, her skin was prickling.

A tiny smile curved Vanessa's blood-red lips. "Believe what you like then… whatever makes you sleep more easily at night."

****

In the light of day, he slept. Sleeping the sleep of the dead. Only he wasn't dead – merely resting, waiting. Soon it would be time to feed again. In his sleep his tongue slithered across his top lip, and a tiny droplet of saliva curdled with undigested blood dripped from his mouth and formed a glistening red gem on the floor.

Chapter Five

Katie was quite glad to bump into Christian again that afternoon. She'd gone into the village to buy a card for Vanessa's birthday, not that she deserved one, thought Katie, as she searched to find one with suitable words.

Eventually coming out of the shop, she spotted Christian sitting on a bench under a shady willow tree. Katie waved. If anyone would know about vampire bats, he would.

"Their normal habitat is Mexico, Brazil, Chile— places like that," Christian said, after Katie had seated herself next to him under the trailing branches and told him about the bat and the calf. "You wouldn't get them in this country, unless it was an escaped illegal pet. I could tell the species if I saw it up close. The problem is, in daylight they're tucked away in some dark shady place."

"Yes, in our attic!" exclaimed Katie, rubbing her arms. It was quite dark and cool under the tree, and she was surprised he wasn't making the most of the sunshine. "If the door had still been there, we could have investigated."

"We still could. Reckon your Granddad's got a ladder?"

Katie stared at him. "You're not suggesting we get

in through the miller's door?"

"Any better ideas?"

"Not really."

"I'll meet you there later if you like," he suggested. "Can't come right now, I've got other things on. About nine this evening?"

"It will be getting dark by then, but if it's the only time you can make it, okay!" Katie agreed. "It's probably best anyway. Granddad will probably be out at a meeting. Somehow, I don't think he'd approve."

"See you later then," he said, smiling and not making an effort to get up from his shady seat.

Katie hesitated. But he obviously wanted her to go and leave him alone. She wouldn't have minded some company. The day stretched long and lonely ahead, so it would have been nice to spend some time with him, chatting, finding things to laugh about. But he remained where he was, settled, with clearly no intention of going anywhere with her.

She fidgeted awkwardly. "I'll see you later then?" "Yes, about nine," he repeated.

She nodded and got up, stepping back out into the sunlight. "See you then."

"See ya!"

She turned and walked away, shaking her head vaguely.

She'd never felt so unpopular in all her life.

Before turning the corner at the top of the street, she

glanced back. He was still sitting there under the shadow of the willow tree. Whatever he had planned for the day clearly wasn't that urgent.

****

Katie really didn't expect Christian to show that evening, nevertheless, she hung around in the garden, pretending to look at the plants. Then, just as the sun was sinking low on the horizon, he appeared.

"All set?" he asked, flashing a cheerful smile.

In one of the sheds, she had earlier found a heavy ladder thick with cobwebs. Getting it up against the side of the house proved a monumental effort, and Katie was exhausted by the time it was lodged firmly into place.

Christian tested the first few rungs. "Safe enough, I reckon."

"Be careful!" Katie warned, looking up at the doorway high above them.

"I'll be okay. I've quite a head for heights anyway."

She clung onto the base as he climbed, feeling the ladder bow and bend the higher he went. Finally, he reached the miller's door and gave it a tug.

"Seems to be bolted from the inside," he called down. "Wood's a bit rotten, though. I could probably make a hole big enough to shine a torch through."

"You do, and you'll pay for it!" came a cold and familiar voice. Vanessa came around the side of the

54

house and stood there looking furious. "What the devil is he doing up there?"

"Looking for bats," Christian shouted down. "Don't worry, I wasn't really going to gouge a hole in your woodwork. In fact, there's a little crack, I could see through if I had a torch. You haven't got one I could borrow, have you?"

Two red spots appeared on Vanessa's white cheeks. "Get down!" she screeched. "Get down this minute before I knock you down!"

"He's not doing any harm," Katie argued, startled by her cousin's outburst.

But Vanessa wouldn't be calmed. She ran at Katie, pushing her aside. Then grabbing the ladder she began to shake it violently. Christian yelled and clung onto the ledge.

"Stop it!" Katie cried, trying to calm her crazed cousin. "Stop it! You'll kill him!"

"Get down then!" she raged. "Now! You're trespassing! Get down now!"

"Okay, okay, I'm coming," Christian gasped, starting his descent while Katie clung to the ladder to try and stop it swaying. Vanessa stood aside, breathing raggedly.

When Christian was back on the ground, Katie glared at her cousin. "That was a terrible thing to do. He could have fallen."

"So, it'll teach you both a lesson," she snapped.

"Keep your noses out of things that don't concern you!"

With that she stormed back into the house, but Katie wasn't standing for it. She raced after her.

"Have you any idea of how dangerous that was? Christian could have broken his neck if he'd fallen. Are you mad or what?"

Vanessa swung round at her. "He had no right being up the ladder, peering in where he's not wanted. Who is he anyway?"

"He's just a boy who's interested in bats, and he certainly didn't deserve to be treated like that! Just what has got into you, Vanessa? What's happened to you? You used to be so nice..."

"Oh, shut up!" Vanessa shrieked as she stalked down the hallway. "Just shut up and leave me alone."

"I won't," Katie shouted back. "You're my cousin. You used to be my friend. I want to know what's going on..."

"Enough!" came a bellow from the study doorway. Granddad stood there, puffed out like a sergeant major. "Stop this arguing. I won't have it. Vanessa was quite right in getting rid of the boy. He has no business prying around our property."

Katie couldn't believe her ears. He was actually sticking up for Vanessa. "Granddad, you didn't see what she did. Christian was right at the top of the ladder and she tried to shake him off. She could have killed him."

"That's enough!" he raged. "She was quite within her rights to get him down before he did any damage."

"But he wasn't doing any damage," Katie argued, her stomach tying itself in a knot. "We were just looking for bats."

"Well, you're not to!" he ranted, his face turning purple. "Do I make myself clear? And if you disobey me, you'll go straight home, regardless of whether your mother is in hospital or not."

Tears sprang into Katie's eyes as Vanessa ran up to her room, no doubt pleased with herself. Granddad turned and marched into his study, having said his piece. But Katie couldn't let it lie. She followed him in.

"Granddad, you can't let her get away with that. If Christian hadn't clung onto the ledge he'd have fallen. He'd probably be dead by now. Is that what you'd want – a boy's death on your hands?"

The old man had his back to her, but it was as if her words had speared him through the heart. He became rigid; his hands turned into tight fists and jerked up to his chest. He started to gasp.

Horrified, Katie suddenly realised he was having another attack.

"Granddad…Granddad…are you all right?" She dragged a chair out from behind his desk and lowered him into it. His face was purple, and his lips had turned blue. "Vanessa!" Katie shouted. "Help me!"

His breath came in short rasping gasps and he

began fumbling in his cardigan pocket.

"Your pills?" Katie said quickly. "Here, let me." But being so agitated in her effort to open the shiny pill box, she succeeded in scattering them all across the floor. "No! Oh no!" she cried, fumbling to retrieve one from the carpet, knowing there wasn't a phone in the house to call for an ambulance. She grasped one of the little pills. "I've got one. I've got one, Granddad." She yelled again for her cousin, "Vanessa! Help me, it's Granddad!"

She slipped the pill under his tongue.

He clung onto her hand his words barely audible. "Katie…Katie, I've done a terrible, terrible thing…"

"Shush, don't try to speak," Katie fretted, loosening his collar. He was sweating, but to her relief as the pill got to work, his colour became lighter, more normal. Gradually his lips turned from blue back to pink. His breathing relaxed.

Realising he was going to be alright, Katie sank exhausted down at his feet. Vanessa still hadn't made an appearance.

Minutes later, his hand fell lightly onto her shoulder. "Thank you," he said quietly. "Would you gather up the pills we scattered? I'm no good without my pills."

"Yes, of course," she replied, crawling around the room, collecting as many as she could find.

"Now I think I'll go and lie down."

Later when he was settled, Katie went shakily back outside. She didn't expect Christian to have hung around, yet there he was, sitting on a tree stump in the twilight.

She ran over to him. "Christian, I'm so sorry."

To her relief he grinned. "Well, I gather the attic is strictly off limits. They brick one entrance up and guard the other with your crazy cousin."

Katie shook her head. "I don't understand why she reacted like that."

"Maybe she's got something to hide up there."

"Such as?"

He shrugged. "Who knows? Could be a dead body, for all we know."

"It could well be, judging by the way she carried on!" Katie agreed, giving him an uncertain little smile. "I should make you a coffee or something, it's the least I can do after almost getting you killed, only I don't think you'd be very welcome."

"Don't worry, I won't go where I'm not invited."

"But I feel terrible. I almost got you killed."

"It's okay…Please don't worry. You've got enough on your plate without worrying about me – your mom's in the hospital, your cousin is a nutcase…" He pulled a face, "Can't wait to meet your grandfather. What's he, a homicidal maniac?"

"No, he just shouts a lot. I think basically he's a good man."

Christian gave her a puzzled look. "You don't sound too sure."

That was because his words had suddenly jumped into her head: *Katie, I've done a terrible, terrible thing.*

****

Granddad's comment of doing a terrible thing was still troubling Katie as she went downstairs the following morning. Her appetite had deserted her, which she was glad of, as the last thing she felt like was sitting down to breakfast with her cousin.

She was relieved to see her granddad was up and about though, no worse for his angina attack last night. He was in no mood for talking either, as he took a plate of toast and a cup of tea into his study and snapped the door shut.

At least the weather had brightened, Katie realised as she went outside. The sun was shining and there was barely a cloud in the sky. Heading away from the house, she crossed the deserted lane and wandered into Oatmeal Woods. Demon woodcutters and hobgoblins weren't half as bad as a spiteful cousin and a granddad who had fallen under her power for some reason.

The scents of pine and wild garlic filled the air as the trees closed ranks around her. Underfoot the ground was lush with ferns and tall grasses and clumps of giant mushrooms and toadstools.

But wandering through the woods wasn't much fun without Vanessa making up stories as they went. Katie heaved a sigh, aware that those days were over forever.

Her thoughts flew back to her granddad, and yesterday. It was weird how he'd sided with Vanessa over Christian trying to see into the attic.

She couldn't help wondering if maybe the attic had something to do with the terrible thing he had done.

Perhaps that was it. Maybe he had no choice but to side with her. Maybe Vanessa knew what this terrible thing was. Maybe she was blackmailing him over it. It surely couldn't just be because he'd pushed Nanna. Katie was positive that he wouldn't have hurt her deliberately. Besides, if there'd been any hint of foul play, the doctor who examined Nanna would have discovered it.

No, it couldn't be that—there was something else. Something more sinister. Something so terrible that Vanessa had forced him to change his will over it.

Perhaps he was afraid that she'd tell people. After all, he was a pillar of society. He was highly respected. He was even being considered for Lord Mayor. If people discovered he'd done something terrible, it would bring disgrace down on him. Maybe he'd be thrown off his precious committees. Or maybe it was something so terrible that he would go to prison for it.

Whatever his terrible thing was, Vanessa shared his

secret. And it was something connected to the attic.

It all started to become clear.

That was why they'd bricked up the entrance. It was why Vanessa went berserk when Christian almost saw inside and why Granddad sided with Vanessa about getting Christian down. He didn't want his terrible deed discovered. He'd rather live under its shadow than have people know.

And of course Vanessa went berserk because if someone was to find out, she would lose the power of blackmail. So it wasn't that Vanessa was protecting Granddad when Christian tried to look in the attic. She was protecting her own interests.

Lost in thought, but finally starting to feel like she was getting somewhere, Katie wandered deeper into the woods, blinking as shafts of sunlight glinted down through the trees. Beneath her feet the ground was soft and mossy. Birds sang and twittered overhead, and occasionally a squirrel scampered across her path and disappeared amongst the leafy branches.

Then something straight ahead stopped her dead in her tracks. The bright afternoon sun was sending a shaft of dazzling light through a gap in the overhead leafy canopy. It illuminated the presence of a teenage boy standing there.

Katie caught her breath. He was tall with shoulder length golden hair that shimmered in the sunlight. He looked about seventeen, dressed entirely in white –

white jeans, white shirt.

Standing there, he looked as if he were standing in a spotlight. Like an angel that had slid down the sunbeam to land there in the woods.

Katie's heart was thudding wildly. Partly because of the way he looked, partly because she was well aware of the dangers of being alone in the woods with a stranger.

She quickly changed course and headed towards the lane and the village. Walking briskly, she glanced back over her shoulder. He was still there, standing motionless in the spotlight, and as she looked, she saw his face break into a smile.

She hurried on, heart thudding. When she finally risked a second glance back, he had gone.

So had the ray of sunlight.

And Katie shivered.

Chapter Six

"You're not eating, Katie?"

She pushed the food about on her plate. "I'm not very hungry actually, Granddad."

Sitting between him and Vanessa at the table that evening completely took away her appetite. She felt like an intruder, an unwelcome, uninvited visitor.

They shared some awful secret. Something connected to that attic.

Katie glanced at Vanessa, her white face was barely visible behind her mask of long black hair. Her cold-hearted cousin. What had happened to make her turn against her own relatives?

If Granddad had done something so awful, Vanessa must really hate him to blackmail him over it rather than try to help him. But of course, she did hate him. She blamed him for Nanna dying.

He won't get away with it!

Katie tried to eat something, but her eyes settled on the pale face of her cousin. What had she meant by that? Just what revenge was she planning?

Vanessa suddenly raised her head, her cold eyes fixed on Katie, startling her. "How's your mother?"

Her question completely took her by surprise. Amazed that her cousin was taking an interest, she answered, "She's due to have her operation any time now, but she was asleep when I called, so I didn't get to talk to her."

"No chance of her being out of the hospital before the weekend then?"

The sudden hope that Vanessa actually cared was instantly dashed and Katie answered stiffly, "No, afraid not. Looks like you're stuck with me for a bit longer."

Vanessa shot her a furious look. "You are not going to spoil my party! Granddad, you'll have to find someone to have her for the night. I don't want her here on Saturday. I've been planning this party for months, and I won't have it spoiled!"

Katie's chin crumpled as she pushed back her chair. "I don't want to go to your stupid party! I wouldn't come if you begged me. I'd rather just walk the streets until it's over, that's better than being where I'm not wanted."

Granddad patted her hand. "Katie, it won't come to that. You and I will go into town and see a film or something…"

It was Vanessa's turn to throw back her chair as she jumped to her feet, but her chair went skittering across the kitchen floor. "See! She's spoiling it for me already. Granddad, you *have* to be at my party. You said you'd be there!"

"Yes, but surely you'll have more fun without an old fogey like me there," he said, unable to stop the look of pleasure on his face that she actually wanted him there. It even confused Katie.

Vanessa lowered her voice, sounding almost pleasant. "Granddad, you have to be there. It's my sixteenth. Nanna won't be there, so you have to be."

His moustache bristled. "Well, all right, if it's that important to you."

"It is," she murmured, looking pleased with herself. Then taking some foil from the kitchen drawer, she wrapped her barely touched meal and put it in the fridge. "I'll have this as a midnight snack. I'm going out." Grabbing her long black velvet coat from the peg, she swept out of the house without a backwards glance.

Granddad looked sympathetically at Katie. "I'm sorry she's like this. I think this party idea is stressing her out. I...I'll try and find somewhere for you to go on Saturday evening. I'll ask at my committees."

Katie bit her lip, determined not to cry. Then concentrating solely on the meal in front of her, she forced herself to eat – and not to think.

After washing the plates, she put on her jacket, zipped it up to her chin, and wandered down the garden with Smoky at her heels, pouncing on moths. While the cat went to hunt in the long grass, Katie settled herself on the swing and pulled her collar up, remembering last night all too well. It couldn't have been a vampire bat. You don't have them in this country. It must have been her eyes playing tricks.

She watched the bats as they flitted to and fro,

swooping and dipping, chasing nothing more than the tiny midges that swarmed in the air. She tried to track one of the bats, to see whether it returned to the eaves of the bakehouse, but it was almost impossible not to lose sight of them in the twilight.

But then by chance, just as she was looking in the direction of an old barn, she saw one swoop through the broken windowpane of the ramshackle wooden building. A second later another bat flew out.

She stopped swinging, and sat, stock still, watching as more bats came and went through the barn window. An uncomfortable prickle of unease ran down her spine. The bats lived in the barn.

So what was upstairs in the attic?

Her gaze switched to the miller's doorway. The ladder was gone. She guessed her granddad had put it away again.

There was definitely a dark secret connected to the attic. Just what was it that granddad was so afraid for people to know about?

She couldn't begin to imagine.

Unable to settle, she wandered down the garden to the stile. The cows were lying on the grass, settled for the night. It was dark now and she could just make out their large silhouettes as they rested after a busy day's grazing.

Leaning against the stile, she looked back at the house, smothered in ivy and creepers, as if the undergrowth was slowly smothering everything. She sighed, sad that all the happy times she could remember were gone forever. Behind her, the cows began to moo restlessly. She glanced back to find them all lumbering to their feet, agitated. Her skin began to prickle. Surely it wasn't that revolting bat again?

She clutched the collar of her jacket tightly, peering through the darkness at the shadowy outline of the cattle.

Then she spotted what was frightening them, and her blood ran cold.

Someone was out there. Someone… or something.

A person. A shadowy figure in a flowing cloak or coat, someone almost merging with the night, but not quite.

She backed away from the stile, her heart thudding, her throat dry, gripped with the horrible sensation that if she had to scream for help, she wouldn't be able to utter a sound.

Desperate to get indoors, she tried to run, but her feet slipped on the wet grass and she skidded. Panic welled up inside of her. Something skittered in front of her face – a moth or bat? She fended it off, afraid it was some horrible blood-sucking creature of the night.

Somehow, she managed not to scream. To make a sound would alert the person darting around in the field and maybe draw him this way. And she needed to be as far away from that person…that *thing*, as possible.

It was human – at least in appearance, although it wasn't behaving humanly. As she watched Katie saw that it was prancing and leaping, just like the bat had done, trying to bite the cows' necks.

She was trembling so badly that she doubted her legs would carry her as far as the house. Somehow, she reached the back door and fell in, slamming it shut behind her, shaking as she drew the bolt across.

"Granddad!" she cried, running along the passageway to his study. "Granddad!"

"Katie? Whatever's the matter?"

"Th… there's a… a man or something in the cow field. It looks like he's trying to bite the cows' necks. Granddad, I think it's a vampire!"

He couldn't stop himself from smiling. But he got stiffly up from behind his desk and patted her shoulder reassuringly. "There's no such thing as vampires. You'll probably find it's the farmer. Goodness me, you're trembling."

"What are we going to do?" Katie cried, hanging on to his arm.

"I'll go and see, shall I?" he suggested, heading towards the kitchen.

Katie stayed close behind him. "It might not be safe. He could attack us!"

"Lock yourself in, then, Katie, if you're this frightened, while I check."

But she couldn't do that either. So warily she

followed him out into the darkness, tiptoeing through the long grass to the bottom of the garden.

Amazingly, the cattle appeared to be calm again.

"I can't see anybody, can you?" Granddad murmured, walking the length of the fence. "It all looks quiet now." He called out, "Hello! Is anybody there?"

"I saw somebody, Granddad. I really did."

"Well, he's gone now," he reassured her. "Come along in now, Katie, it's getting late."

The oblong shaft of light from the kitchen shone out across the garden, and Katie gasped. "We left the door open! He could have sneaked in."

For the first time, her granddad looked slightly anxious. He hesitated at the open back door before venturing in, followed closely by Katie. They both heard the rustle of fabric from the hall and, for a second, stood motionless. Katie could literally hear her heart thudding.

And then Vanessa swept into the kitchen, her long black coat swishing against the furniture. She stopped as she came face to face with them. "Hello? What's the matter with you two? You look like you've seen a ghost!"

Katie instantly felt a rush of relief. "It was you, wasn't it?"

Vanessa gave a shrug. "What was me?"

"It was you in the cow field, pretending to be a vampire."

Vanessa uttered a harsh little laugh. "Me? Do I look like a vampire?"

Katie stared at her. With her long black clothes, her jet-black hair and Gothic makeup, she could quite easily be mistaken for a vampire. "You do actually, yes!"

"Well, I'm not," Vanessa dismissed, taking her leftover meal from the fridge and pouring herself a large glass of milk. She raised the glass. "Milk—not blood. But it's funny you should mention vampires. I could have sworn I saw a cloaked figure lurking on the edge of the woods as I came by. I think you should definitely lock and bolt the doors tonight."

"You think you're so clever, don't you!" Katie interrupted her cousin. "I know what you're trying to do."

"Do you really?" Vanessa remarked flippantly.

"Yes, you're trying to scare me away. It's just another little ploy to try and get me to go home before your precious party. Well, you don't frighten me, Vanessa, not one little bit."

Granddad bolted the back door and headed back to his study. "I can see where this conversation is heading, so I shall leave you ladies to your fantasies. I have work to finish."

As soon as he was out of earshot, Katie said quietly, "You might scare Granddad, but you don't scare me."

"I'm not trying to scare you," Vanessa said, drawing the kitchen curtains. "But maybe we should take this a little more seriously. If you saw someone lurking in the cow field and I saw someone hanging around in the woods, maybe we should be careful. I told you the crypt got broken open, didn't I? Perhaps it's that young vampire. Maybe he's out and looking for revenge." She lowered her voice and leaned towards Katie, her icy blue eyes sparkling with mischief. "Maybe he's thirsty for your blood."

A shiver ran down Katie's spine. "Shut up, Vanessa! You're not funny anymore. And another thing, you said it was bats in the attic making those noises. Well, I happen to know the bats live in the barn. I saw them coming and going from there tonight."

Vanessa's eyes hardened. "You're sure about that, are you?"

"Absolutely! So, what is actually making those noises I keep hearing?"

Her cousin shrugged. "Who knows? Maybe it's a ghost or a ghoul. Anyway, you're wrong about the bats."

"No, I'm not, and I'll prove it to you tomorrow. I'm going to take a look in that barn and see for myself."

"Good! You do that," she dismissed. Then swooping down on Katie with her black hair swirling and her white face so close that her perfume was quite overpowering, said, "But let's hope you don't find Dracula himself sleeping in there."

Katie drew back from her cousin, feeling as if her

cousin's creepy words had turned her blood to ice.

Later, Katie sat huddled in her duvet, eyes huge, listening for any squeak or scuffles from above. But the attic was as silent as the grave. Nothing was moving about up there tonight.

Was it possible the bats had moved out, transferred their home from the attic to the shed overnight? Christian would know. He probably knew the habits of all the bat species.

She wished they were on the phone; the house was isolated enough. Although she wasn't so worried about the figure lurking in the cow field now. It must have been Vanessa. She'd done it to scare her. To frighten her into going home before her precious party which was only two days away now. Her precious surprise party. What was it she had said?

Wait and see what the surprise is…

Katie tried to relax and sleep. Tomorrow she would try and find Christian. At least he'd be able to see the bats now. Vanessa wouldn't stop them looking in an old barn, would she?

She closed her eyes, but sleep refused to come. All she could think of was a fleeting shadow scuttling through the darkness, just out of reach.

At last, sleep drifted over her, but it was an unpleasant sleep, filled with nightmares. She dreamed of running along a passageway, running from something – some blood-dripping creature at her heels.

73

Desperate to escape, she burst through a door – only it was a door to nowhere, with a sheer drop below it and she was falling…

She awoke with a start. There'd been a noise, a bang.

She shot out of bed, her heart thudding. Fumbling to find the light switch, she stood in her room, her startled reflection mirrored back from every angle.

It was definitely a bang, like a door slamming. Had someone broken in?

Suddenly there was another bang. This one seemed to come from above Vanessa's bedroom.

Without a second thought, Katie raced along the corridor to Vanessa's room and barged in.

Vanessa was out of bed and standing at her open wardrobe.

Dressed in pyjamas with her face cleansed of her usual dramatic make-up, she looked like the Vanessa Katie knew and loved. Until she opened her mouth.

"Get out of my room!" she shrieked, slamming her wardrobe doors.

"I heard a noise, a bang. Didn't you hear anything?"

Vanessa scowled. "No, I didn't. You must have dreamt it. Go back to bed."

"I didn't dream it…" Katie protested. "Well, maybe the first noise might have been in my sleep, but I was out of bed and wide awake when I heard the second bang. It came from in here. Sort of above you."

"It's bats, I've told you. They're stupid little creatures. They've probably dislodged something up in the attic."

Katie shook her head. "There are no bats up there, Vanessa. The bats live in the barn. Besides, this was a bang."

Vanessa ran her fingers through her hair, her eyes furtive. "A bang, you say? Was it like a door shutting?"

"Yes! Yes, that's it exactly!" Katie exclaimed.

"That was me. I slammed my bedroom door a bit too hard by accident."

"It sounded like it came from the attic. Isn't there a trapdoor in your ceiling?"

Vanessa spread her arms in a gesture of openness. "Can you see one? I've told you, it's these old houses. Sound carries in weird ways sometimes."

"But I really thought I heard two bangs." Puzzled, Katie looked up to find there wasn't a trapdoor in her ceiling at all, although she could have sworn there used to be one in here.

Vanessa ushered her towards the door. "I banged my door twice. It didn't shut the first time. Sorry, didn't mean to wake you. Good night."

The fact that Vanessa had apologised was surprising enough, but before Katie could say another word, she was back out in the corridor, and Vanessa's bedroom door shut in her face.

It closed with a click—not a bang.

Katie returned to her bedroom and slid back into bed, knowing she would never get to sleep now.

The silence of the old house lasted for hours. She lay, wide awake listening. It must have been around four in the morning when she heard more sounds coming from the attic.

Only this time it wasn't bangs.

It was whispering.

Chapter Seven

In the light of day he slept. Hiding from the sunlight, waiting for the darkness..

Soon it would be time to feed again. He savoured the moment and saliva curdled with undigested blood and seeped from the corner of his mouth.

****

Katie sat at the kitchen table, watching raindrops chase each other down the windowpane. It would probably only be a shower, as already the clouds were breaking up and the sun was starting to peep through again, promising a fine day.

Granddad had gone into town early on business. There was no sign of Vanessa.

Try as she might, Katie couldn't get last night out of her mind. Bangs, whisperings, secrets. Something only Vanessa and Granddad knew about.

Their sinister secret.

Katie jumped as Vanessa suddenly swept into the house, soaked. Her long black hair clung to her face like rats' tails.

"You look half-drowned," Katie remarked. "I didn't think it was raining that hard."

Vanessa flapped her long black skirt to stop it from

clinging to her legs. "It's not now. I've been out ages." She looked directly at Katie, a secretive expression on her white face. "Things to do, you know."

"I heard someone whispering last night," Katie said bluntly, watching her cousin's face for any tell-tale signs, but she merely arched her eyebrows disinterestedly.

"After the bangs," Katie continued. "I lay awake for hours then I heard someone whispering."

Vanessa shook her head. "You won't believe me, but I've told you, we have bats in the attic, and this is an old house, remember. It creaks and groans."

"The bats live in a barn," Katie reminded her.

"Maybe there's more than one colony of bats. Have you considered that?" Vanessa dismissed, turning her back on Katie to make herself a coffee.

"If there is, they weren't out last night."

"Beats me, then." Vanessa shrugged as if it really didn't bother her one way or the other. "Maybe there is a ghost lurking in the attic after all! How's your mother, by the way – had her op yet?"

"Possibly today, I'm not sure," Katie answered, under no delusion that her cousin actually cared. Vanessa had changed the subject on purpose.

"You should go and visit her."

"I wish I could," Katie said truthfully. She longed to be back home with her mum and school friends. Anything rather than being stuck here with – what was it Christian had called her? Her crazy cousin!

"Don't let me stop you," Vanessa said, pouring herself a huge bowl of cereal.

Katie lowered her eyes, hiding the misery inside. It hurt that Vanessa was so hostile. She badly needed a friend now that her mum was so ill. What if she didn't pull through? What if she was stuck here with Vanessa and Granddad forever? She banished the thought from her head. Her mum would get better. She had to.

Concentrating on her plans for the day, she asked, "Have you any objection to me looking for bats in the barn? You're not going to come ranting and raging again, are you?"

"If you want to go rummaging around in a filthy old barn, carry on," she remarked, looking down her elegant nose. "Is Bat Boy going too?"

"If I happen to bump into him, I'll see if he wants to, although I doubt he'd ever want to set foot in our garden ever again."

"Well, he shouldn't go poking his nose in where it isn't wanted," said Vanessa, sweeping out of the kitchen to eat her breakfast upstairs.

Katie heaved a sigh. It saddened her to see how nasty and spiteful Vanessa had become.

Once it had stopped raining, Katie went out into the garden and headed for the barn. It was a shame Christian wasn't around. He'd probably be quite excited about seeing a colony of bats up close.

She half expected the barn door to have seized up, as it must have been years since anyone used it, but the creaky old door opened quite easily on its rusty hinges. Instantly a shaft of sunlight sliced through the gloom, and a million dust particles danced in its rays.

The barn was cluttered with old milling machinery and boxes of junk piled high. Old flour sacks hung over the roof beams, and the floor was cluttered with the remnants of a once-busy flour mill.

There was little room to move, but Katie picked her way through the clutter, quite excited now at the prospect of finding a colony of sleeping pipistrelle bats. She was positive that's what they were. The prancing bat couldn't have been a vampire bat. It must have been her imagination, brought on by having a cousin like Vanessa.

She spotted them easily. A dozen or more small brown creatures hanging upside down from a rafter, their paper-thin wings wrapped around their little bodies. Eagerly she climbed over more junk to get closer. To her side, a large sheet of dark leathery canvas was draped from another low beam. She accidentally nudged it with her arm as she clambered over some boxes.

It moved.

It moved of its own accord.

Katie stopped dead in her tracks. Her eyes swivelled left, a cloying sensation of alarm churning in the pit of her stomach.

Slowly, she risked another look. The canvas was folded, wrapped inward on itself. Almost two meters in length—a strange kind of canvas. It had a vein-like pattern all over it.

Then, to her horror, she saw that it wasn't actually draped over anything at all. Two clawed feet, like grotesque monster feet from a fancy-dress shop, were hooked over the wooden beam from which it dangled.

Horrified, her eyes slowly scanned the long length of its body to its base and there she saw a head – half rodent, half human, with two sharp bat ears.

Her petrified scream shook the dust from the rafters and two bulbous eyes opened wide.

Katie fled.

She tore into the house, screaming for her cousin. "Vanessa! Vanessa! Come down! There's something in the barn...Vanessa!" Her last cry came out as a sob as her cousin finally came dawdling downstairs.

Katie couldn't speak. Not at first, then grabbing Vanessa's arm, she practically pulled her out of the house. "You've got to see..."

"Will you stop it, you idiot!" Vanessa yelled, writhing free.

"In the barn," Katie stammered, giving her cousin a push. "A giant bat! A monster! Please! Just go and look."

With a backward glance that told Katie her cousin

thought she'd gone completely crazy, Vanessa sauntered into the barn.

Katie clung onto the back door, ready to slam it shut if that thing should come flying out.

But nothing came swooping out of the barn, and there were no screams from Vanessa as the minutes ticked by. Finally, Vanessa wandered out from behind the old wooden doors and stood with her hands on her hips.

"What am I supposed to be looking for?"

"A…a thing. A monstrous bat…bigger than me…" Her words died away as realisation dawned.

It was a trick. Another of Vanessa's tricks. That's what she'd been doing all morning, setting it up. The horrific mask and feet could have been in that package she'd had delivered the other day. Those eyes were probably painted table tennis balls.

"Don't you ever give up trying to scare me to death, Vanessa?" Katie asked in despair, her eyes fluttering shut in exasperation. "Okay, I'm impressed! This was much scarier than you prancing around in a cow field pretending to be Dracula."

Vanessa cast her a scathing glance as she swept back into the kitchen. "I haven't a clue what you're talking about. Now if you don't mind, I've a party to organise."

Katie sank down onto a chair, wondering just how far her cousin would go to force her out of here. Was she that desperate to make sure she was long gone before her precious surprise party?

Knowing there'd be no sign of the monster bat now, Katie went back into the barn. The pipistrelles were still there, but no hideous giant bat. A dark sheet of canvas lay crumpled on the floor, near where the giant bat had been. Katie tried to think whether it had been there before. It didn't seem to have the same veined texture, but she couldn't be sure. She searched for a while, trying to find the mask and clawed feet, but there was so much junk.

Besides, she didn't need actual proof. She knew it was Vanessa playing her spiteful tricks. There was no other explanation.

****

Despite everything, Katie bought her spiteful cousin a little birthday present for tomorrow – a new mascara. Judging by the amount she used, she probably went through it by the bucket-load.

If they'd still been friends, she would have bought her something more special, like a bracelet. But sadly, there was no love lost between them anymore.

Her next job was to call the hospital from the phone box. After quite a long wait and a variety of different voices in the background, she was finally connected to her mum. She'd had her operation, but she sounded weak and drowsy. Katie prayed it was the effects of her anesthetic, and not because her mum was deteriorating after her operation.

Katie kept the conversation light, determined not to worry her about the awful time she was having with Vanessa and Granddad. After a few minutes her mum sounded really sleepy, so Katie told her to get some rest and that she would call her again tomorrow.

She walked blindly out of the phone booth and straight into a teenage boy carrying an armful of books. The books went flying in all directions.

"Oh! I'm sorry!" exclaimed Katie, stooping to help him pick them up. They were library books – big adventure novels.

"No worries! Oh, hello!"

Katie looked into his face. It was him, the angel in the sunbeam. "Oh! Hi!"

"You're Vanessa's cousin, aren't you? I saw you in the woods the other day."

"Yes, that's right," Katie answered, amazed that he'd remembered seeing her. And even more amazed to discover he knew who she was.

"How's your mum?"

"She's…er…okay, I think. She's just coming around from her operation. How did you know?"

"I'm a friend of your cousin. She mentioned you were staying with her."

"Yes, I bet," Katie murmured, noticing what brilliant blue eyes he had – an unusual deep ocean blue.

His smile was sympathetic, as if making excuses for Vanessa. "She misses her grandma, you know. She was like a mother to her."

"So she takes her misery out on Granddad and me?" Katie blurted out, instantly regretting her outburst, feeling totally disloyal. Vanessa was her cousin, after all.

His blue eyes softened, as if he understood what she was going through. "Be patient. She's not all bad. She's just got to get it out of her system."

"Has she really?" Katie murmured, wondering if he'd be so understanding if he knew about all the nasty tricks she'd played and how awful she was to their granddad.

He didn't say any more. He just smiled and said, "Anyway, I've got to be going. See you around, maybe."

"Yes, okay...enjoy your books."

"I will."

Katie watched him go, realising there was one thing in Vanessa's favour: she had one very loyal friend.

Later, when she had no option but to go back to the bakehouse for dinner, she realised that Vanessa also had one very loyal granddad. Following the aroma into the kitchen, she found her granddad busy at the cooker.

"Is that beef casserole I can smell?"

"Got to feed the troops!" he said, puffing out his chest. "Although I've noticed you don't eat enough to feed a sparrow, whereas Vanessa eats like a horse." He nodded his white head towards a cardboard box. "I've bought a birthday cake for tomorrow. Have a look."

Katie opened the cake box. The cake was all white icing and sugared flowers. She smiled. "That's lovely, Granddad. She'll love it!" Although, deep down, Katie guessed Vanessa wouldn't give her granddad as much as a thank you for making the effort.

"I hope so," he murmured more to himself than anyone.

"I've got her a card and a new mascara. It's not much but..." She let her words trail away, guessing he'd understand why she hadn't made much of an effort. "Have you got her anything?"

"Well, not as such," he said, casting a rueful little smile that barely concealed his sadness over their situation. "I was informed that all she wants from me is money."

Katie squeezed his hand impulsively. "Granddad, you could come back with me when Mum's better. You don't have to stay here with her."

He smiled wistfully. "I have my committees here, and what if I should become Lord Mayor? The election is tomorrow, you know."

"Think about it, anyway," Katie urged. "You're not trapped here with Vanessa. You could sell the house while it's still yours to sell."

His eyes suddenly brightened, as if the idea had never occurred to him. Then almost as quickly the spark died. Katie knew instinctively that Vanessa was standing in the doorway, listening.

She swept in, filling the room with her perfume. Her eyes narrowed to black slits. "Charming! Sell my home from under me. Well, go ahead, Granddad, I can't stop you. It's still yours legally while you're alive. It doesn't become mine until you're dead!"

"Vanessa!" Katie cried, horrified by her cousin's callousness. The older girl tossed back her hair. "I'm only stating facts."

"You're only being despicable!" Katie shot at her, then turned to her granddad, pleading with him, "Don't put up with this, Granddad. Don't let her treat you like this."

A half smile twisted Vanessa's pale features. "It's your choice, Granddad. I'll leave it up to you. Oh, it is tomorrow that they elect the new mayor, isn't it? People must think very highly of you. It would be such a shame to disappoint them, wouldn't it?"

The old man began to crumple. His shoulders hunched, his hands trembled, and he fumbled for a pill as Vanessa swept out of the room.

Katie put her arm around him. "She can't do this to you, Granddad. It's blackmail."

"I'm a selfish old man," he uttered, slipping a pill under his tongue. "A weak, selfish old man."

"No, you're not! You're a caring man. Look at all the time you give to your committees and things. You care about other people, Granddad. I know you do."

"Do I?" he murmured, his eyes misty with tears. "Maybe it's my own self-importance that I care about."

"I don't believe that for a moment."

He shook his head miserably. "You don't know me, Katie, not really."

He fell silent then and as the pill began to work, Katie sat down beside him and quietly watched what little colour he had in his face return. Eventually he patted her hand. "Would you dish up some dinner for yourself? I'm not that hungry now. I think I'm going to have a bit of a lie-down."

As Katie watched him shuffle out of the room, she wished she knew what was going on here. First, he said he'd done a terrible, terrible thing and now he thought of himself as a weak, selfish old man. If only he'd share this awful secret with her, she might be able to help.

She ate alone, which suited her, and then because she couldn't settle and watch TV, she took a walk back down into the village. She hoped she might bump into Christian. Not only that, she was only too aware that she needed to find something to do tomorrow evening when the party was on.

Lots of people were out strolling and enjoying the warm summer's evening, some walking their dogs, others with their babies and toddlers. Katie ambled along, lost in thought, taking her time. She had a whole evening to fill.

The fine weather had brought lots of locals out and the village was buzzing. A game of cricket was being played on the village green, and Katie sat on a park bench and watched for a while.

Growing bored of that, she passed away some time in the library. On her way out, she spotted a poster advertising an illustrated talk on bats at the village hall the following evening. Katie made a note of the time. It would be better than nothing, and Christian might even be there too.

She emerged from the library to find the sun had gone down and twilight was casting its magical glow over everything. She walked briskly back through the village and up the lane leading home. No one was about now. The lane was deserted.

Katie quickened her step, keeping to the outer edges of the pavement, away from the trees. The woods didn't hold the same appeal now that she and Vanessa were no longer friends. It had been a fun, exciting place to play when there were two of them, making up stories, enjoying the fresh air and wildlife. Now it just looked dark and uninviting.

A sound behind her made her spin around. She jumped to find someone loping up the lane towards her. He had a strangerun, all arms and legs, not at all athletic, more comic. But she didn't feel like laughing. Vanessa's tales about someone lurking in the woods might have just been fantasy, but it still made her nervous when there was no one else about.

And then she saw who it was and heaved a sigh of relief. "Christian!"

"Slow down!" he called out. "You walk faster than I run."

"Hi." Katie smiled, pleased to see a friendly face.

He jogged breathlessly alongside her. "Great to see you. How's your mum?"

"Well, she had her op today," Katie told him. "But she sounded really tired when I spoke to her earlier."

"That's the effects of the anesthetic," he said with a nod, falling into step beside her. "And how's the cousin from hell?"

"As awful as ever," Katie groaned. "Oh, you'll never believe the trick she played on me this morning."

He looked intrigued and his dark eyes seemed to glow in the twilight. "What did she do?"

"Well, I discovered that the bats are living in the barn, not in the attic at all. And she knew I intended taking a look in the barn, just out of interest, so she rigged up a giant bat monstrosity and hung it from a beam. Honestly, I nearly had a heart attack. It opened its eyes and everything!"

Christian shook his head. "She's a real head case, that cousin of yours."

"I know. And earlier, she'd pretended to be a vampire and went flapping and swooping around in the cow field. She must have known I was in the back

90

garden and would see her. She's just a lunatic. All this to persuade me to go home before her stupid party tomorrow."

"You'll be glad to go home then?" Christian said, looking just a little disappointed.

"I will, yes. Just as soon as Mum's out of hospital they won't see me for dust." She saw him gaze off into the distance, and realised how unkind that must have sounded, as if she couldn't care less about him as a new friend. "It's been great meeting you though. Maybe we could keep in touch."

"Maybe," he agreed, vaguely.

She felt quite awful for a moment, and then thought what would cheer him up. "Hey! Would you like to see the bats, now that I know where they live?"

"I'd love to, only they'll be out feeding now. Besides, I'm not exactly welcome in your granddad's home, am I?"

"You'd be there on my invitation," Katie said determinedly. "If they don't like it, that's just their hard luck!"

He looked doubtful. "Are you sure? I won't go where I'm not invited."

"I'm inviting you!" Katie insisted. "You're very welcome in my granddad's house – at least while I'm staying there."

He smiled that familiar white smile. "Thank you. I'll remember that. Only right now I've got to get off for a bite to eat. I'll walk you back home first though."

"Thanks." She smiled, glad to have some pleasant company up the long, lonely lane.

They chatted away like old friends, and she told him about the talk on bats tomorrow. He seemed interested. By the time they said goodnight, Katie was feeling so much happier.

Crossing the lane to the bakehouse, she spotted Smoky. He had a little creature in his mouth. Katie hurried after him, guessing it was a mouse and she was anxious to save it, if it wasn't too late.

Smoky had other ideas, however, and darted around the side of the house, disappearing into the shrubbery. She raced after him, scrambling around the bushes until finally coming face-to-face with a pair of luminous eyes watching her from the undergrowth.

"Smoky, you bad cat. What have you caught?"

It looked like a little field mouse, but Katie could see straightaway that she was already too late to save its life. "Oh Smoky, did you have to? Poor little thing."

Smoky, however, looked proud of his catch and padded proudly away into the darkness like a mighty hunter with its prey.

Katie went to stand up, when a movement caught her eye.

She stopped, still crouched in the shrubs, motionless, except for her heart, which seemed to have leapt into her mouth.

Someone was creeping along behind the barn.

She shrank back into the undergrowth, her throat tight with fear, her heart racing.

The shadowy figure vanished for a moment behind the barn and she stared, barely daring to blink, waiting for it to emerge.

And then it did. It was a man—or someone dressed like a man; she was only too aware that Vanessa could be up to her tricks again.

He moved with stealth, crouched low. Then suddenly he turned to face the wall beneath the miller's doorway, merging with the night and the dark creeping ivy that smoothed the brickwork.

Katie watched, barely blinking, but couldn't believe her eyes as he reached up and grabbed hold of the creeping ivy…and began to climb.

Effortlessly his feet found footholds. Hand over hand he scaled the sheer wall, moving swiftly, easily, as if he'd done this a hundred times before.

Katie clasped her hands over her mouth, stifling her scream as he skittered like some horrendous giant bat up to the miller's door, arms and legs moving in precise rhythm, climbing the vertical wall as easy as climbing the stairs.

She wanted to scream. Instead she crouched there, hands clasped tightly over her mouth watching in utter horror and disbelief as he…or it, reached the miller's doorway and eased it open, just a little, just enough to slither inside.

And then, without a sound, the door swung shut behind him.

It was over in seconds, as if it had never happened.

In fact, if she hadn't been delayed in going indoors by chasing after Smoky, she would never have known. Now everything was calm and still and silent. Except for inside Katie's head, where a silent scream erupted in her brain.

Something was living in the attic!

Something that looked human but climbed like a bat, was living in the attic.

Man….bat…what did that tell her? Her thoughts raced.

What was it Vanessa had been saying? A Dracula-type figure had been seen in the woods? And then there was that person in the cow field, trying to bite the cow's throats. The broken crypt door – someone had broken in—or broken out.

She clung to the gnarled trunk of a tree for support as her legs threatened to give way. Panic rose inside of her, a desperate, choking sensation, rising up through her stomach into her throat. One word echoing around and around in her head…

Vampire!

Chapter Eight

She had to warn Granddad and Vanessa. She started to run towards the house, then stopped abruptly. Shock waves tearing through her.

Maybe they knew!

Maybe that was why they bricked up the entrance to the attic – to stop him getting into the house.

But why keep it secret? It was horrendous. It needed to be exposed. To be got rid of, somehow. And surely it was no reason for Vanessa to be blackmailing her granddad. It didn't make sense.

Shaking with fear, Katie crept silently towards the house, her eyes not wavering from the miller's door high up in the wall.

What if he decided to come out again?

She was shivering now, even though the evening was mild.

The back door of the bakehouse suddenly seemed an awful long way away. The long silent garden felt eerie. Shadowy trees and bushes crowded the garden where more of these creatures could be lurking.

She couldn't be sure there was only one of them in her attic. What if there was a colony of creeping, climbing monstrosities?

She didn't want to be out in the dark on her own. She wanted desperately to be safe indoors. Only indoors wasn't safe either.

She had no choice, and she darted across the garden, keeping clear of the shadows. Her eyes were wide, glancing this way and that, half expecting someone to lunge at her at any moment—Dracula or some other horror.

She ran the last few steps to the kitchen door and locked it after her. But as she turned the key, she realised the futility of her action. The horror was already in the house with her.

She crept through the downstairs rooms, keeping her voice low. "Granddad, are you in? Granddad?"

Silence greeted her.

Ears straining against the quiet of the old house, she tip-toed up the stairs, hating the prospect of getting closer to the top of the house where that thing was hiding. She tapped her cousin's bedroom door.

"Vanessa!" she called, softly at first, then her voice rose. "Vanessa!"

When no answer came, Katie peeped in. The room was deserted. She checked out all the other rooms before going back downstairs. There was no sign of her cousin, but there was definitely someone standing at the front door, trying to get in.

Her heart thudded as the door opened. Her granddad stepped in.

"Oh, it's you, thank goodness!" she cried, throwing her arms around him.

"Katie, whatever's the matter?"

"There's something in the attic…someone…"

He staggered. "What…what do you mean?"

Wide-eyed, she garbled out what she had seen. "A man, or something like a man. He climbed the outside wall. He just went straight up it, like a spider or a lizard! He went in through the miller's door."

He seemed to relax and gave a little laugh. "I think you're seeing things, Katie. The miller's door is bolted from the inside. Has been for many a year."

"Then it can be just as easily unbolted from the inside. Honestly, Granddad, I saw someone going in there. He…it…is in the attic right now. Right this minute. It explains the noises.

Vanessa said she heard noises too. She blamed bats but it's not bats—it's this thing!"

"No, you're wrong," Granddad cut her short. "It must have been a shadow, a passing car sending its headlights across the building."

"It was nothing like that!" she cried. "I saw him first by the sheds. I watched him. Believe me, Granddad, there's someone up there and we've got to do something!"

"The best thing you can do," said Vanessa suddenly, appearing at the top of the stairs, dressed in black jeans and a black top, "is to stop getting hysterical before you bring on one of Granddad's attacks."

Katie spun around. "Where did you spring from?

You weren't there a minute ago."

"I was in the bathroom."

"I looked in the bathroom."

"Then I must have just come out of the bathroom," she snapped, irritated.

Katie just stared. She hadn't been upstairs a moment ago. So where had she come from?

Granddad seemed to be making light of her fears. "Katie thinks she saw someone climbing the outside wall and going into the attic by the miller's door."

"The door's bolted," Vanessa dismissed. "You'd know better than anyone, seeing as your friend Bat Boy Christian tried to open it the other day."

Christian...

A cold tingling sensation crawled up her spine. They'd first met in the crypt...

"Is she all right?" Vanessa asked her granddad icily, staring at Katie.

Katie looked straight through her, barely seeing her. Seeing instead a hunched shadow, darting around the cow field. Could that have been Christian?

"Christian," she breathed.

"What about him?" Vanessa demanded.

The colour drained from Katie's face. "It's him!"

Her granddad looked anxious suddenly; his skin had turned an unhealthy ashen shade. "You think... you think the boy's got into the attic?" He began to tremble. "You mean he's actually up there, in the attic…?"

Vanessa seemed delighted with the idea. Her mouth curled into an unpleasant smile. "Ah yes, Bat Boy. And you reckon he's up there now, do you, Katie? Granddad won't like that, not one little bit. Will you, Granddad? You don't like boyfriends being upstairs, do you?"

Katie stared at her cousin, wondering what on earth she was on about.

But she hadn't finished. Like a drama queen she descended the stairs slowly and purposefully, accentuate her words with each step. "Well, can you imagine that, Granddad? Bat Boy up there in the attic, poking around, looking to see what he can see. Looking for bats, I imagine, but I don't think he'll find any, do you, Granddad?" There was a wicked glint in her spiteful eyes. "But I wonder what he will stumble across?"

"That's not what I meant…" Katie began, but she saw her granddad was getting into a state again. The old man began to gasp as the colour drained completely from his face and his lips turned a horrible shade of blue.

With trembling hands, he fumbled for a pill, but he was shaking so badly he couldn't get the lid off the pill box.

"Granddad!" Katie cried, holding onto him as his knees buckled. He was heavy and it took all her strength to stop him collapsing onto the floor. "Vanessa, help me!"

But Vanessa stood with her hands on her hips, a cold expression on her white face.

"Vanessa!" Katie screamed as she struggled to get him onto a kitchen chair and managed to get a pill under his tongue. "Get a doctor, this is a bad one."

"The phone's not working, I told you," Vanessa replied vaguely.

"Then run to a neighbour or into the village," she begged, loosening his collar and tie as he gasped for breath.

"Stop panicking." Vanessa shrugged. "He'll be fine once the pill starts working. Besides, I can't leave you alone with an intruder in the house, can I?"

"Just get some help!" Katie cried.

Vanessa stood over him, arms folded. "I suppose I could go and telephone. But I think I'd better phone for the police too and tell them to come and get that intruder out of our attic." She stared innocently at the old man. "Well, Granddad, shall I call the doctor and the police?"

His breathing became shorter, until he was gasping for air.

He shook his head feebly.

"Either fetch a doctor or shut up and leave him alone!" Katie cried. "You're making him worse."

"Don't blame me. You started it," Vanessa said,

tossing back her hair as she skipped back upstairs, leaving them both to it.

Katie glared after her. That girl was despicable.

It was some time before her granddad was well enough to be helped upstairs to bed. The pill eventually did the trick, and once he was settled, Katie made him a cup of tea and stayed with him until he fell asleep.

Exhausted, she went downstairs again and sank onto the sofa. Vanessa was totally heartless. It wouldn't surprise her if it had been her climbing up the wall. Maybe she'd done it to fool their granddad, but that still didn't explain how she could blackmail him over it.

She rubbed her aching forehead. Was she doing Christian an injustice in thinking it could have been him climbing into the attic? But what if it was him? What did that make him?

A boy fascinated by bats—or a young vampire from the seventeenth century?

Her thoughts still raced. If it was Christian, simply being nosy by climbing up the wall, how could he possibly get in through the miller's doorway? It was bolted from the inside.

So, whoever it was, they had control of whether it was bolted or unbolted. They came and went as they pleased.

Katie was brought abruptly out of her thoughts by the scent of perfume.

Vanessa in a long floating black dressing gown

swept along the passageway and into the kitchen.

Furious, Katie raced after her. "How could you!"

Vanessa's face was hidden by her long black hair. "I need a coffee."

"You really couldn't care less about making him ill, could you? He could have died then, and you wouldn't have cared a bit!"

"I don't need this." She shrugged, spooning coffee into a mug, and Katie caught a glimpse of her face. Her eyes looked red and puffy, as if she'd been crying – although Katie really couldn't imagine her cousin crying over anything these days. "Granddad's all right, isn't he?" Vanessa asked dully, concentrating on making her drink.

"Do you honestly care?" Katie asked, sensing a slight change in her cousin, remorse maybe?

But the brashness came back with a vengeance. "Well, I should hate him to have a fatal attack tonight with it being my sixteenth birthday tomorrow. I've gone to so much trouble to organise my surprise party. It would be a terrible shame if anything went wrong now. I'm so looking forward to seeing my efforts come to fruition, so to speak."

No! There was no change in her cousin's hard-hearted attitude. If she had been crying, it wasn't over the fact that their granddad had almost died.

Unable to bear being in the same room as her a moment longer, Katie stormed from the room, saying,

"Well, I won't be at your party. And if your friends are anything like you, you're all welcome to each other."

She stopped abruptly on the bottom step, a cold shiver running up her spine and a dreadful nervousness seeping through her from the pit of her stomach. She would be getting closer to that thing in the attic. She tiptoed, terrified that something was about to leap out at her from some dark alcove at any second.

Her ears were strained for sounds, and every creak spoke of terror and monsters. Somehow, she reached her bedroom, and barricaded herself in as best she could. The dressing table was too heavy to push in front of the door, but a linen chest and a chair would at least make it more difficult for someone to get in if they tried. She knew she wouldn't be able to sleep, and she knew something else too: under no circumstances was she going to spend another night under this roof.

She would leave, tomorrow, on the next train home. She would get as far away from here as possible. She'd go home. Alone in her own empty house was a million times better than being here with Granddad and Vanessa. And safer too.

Her plan sorted in her head. She would pack her things. She wouldn't tell either of them what she was planning on doing. Although Vanessa would be delighted, but her granddad would stick by his duty of looking after her and stop her from going. Under no circumstances did Katie intend spending a minute longer than necessary here.

But for now, she somehow had to get through the night, knowing that hideous monstrosity was creeping about in the attic above her head.

She set about packing, working methodically, trying not to make a sound. Seeing her anxious face reflected back from every angle from the dressing table and wardrobe mirrors.

It was a sultry night and Katie was uncomfortable and hot by the time she'd finished. She opened the top window a little before getting into bed, although she had no intention of sleeping.

For a long time she sat up straight in her bed, pillows plumped up behind her, afraid to sleep, listening for sound from the attic. Every now and then she heard something, like the attic floorboards creaking as if someone was creeping around up there.

She wanted to shout out, "Christian, is that you up there?" But of course, if it was, then it wasn't Christian at all. It was some demonic figure from the seventeenth century.

She tried to recall the name etched into the crypt's stone. At least it hadn't been Christian; she would have remembered. She racked her brains—until it came to her.

Knight! William Knight.

For the want of something better to do, she reached for a pen and notepad from her bag, and doodled the name, seeing what words she could make from the letters.

Within moments she had written the word: killing... and then: I am killing.

With a gasp, she scrunched the sheet of paper up and threw it across her bedroom floor. She needed to be away from here.

Tomorrow couldn't come soon enough.

Chapter Nine

Under a cloak of darkness, he crept through the night, sucking blood. His tongue slowly curled over the two sharp incisors, licking the red droplets. How sweet they tasted. But his needs were fierce; the blood of animals was no substitute for human blood.

The time had come.

He would take the risk...

****

Katie must have nodded off because she awoke with a jolt. The sudden movement caused her wardrobe door to swing open.

As her heart leapt into her mouth, she sprang out of bed and banged it shut, terrified that Dracula himself was about to leap out. Her heart was hammering as she tried to console herself by recalling that she hadn't jammed the door shut with cardboard.

That's why it opened — nothing else. Even so, she couldn't bring herself to close her eyes again.

At one o'clock Katie was still sitting on the edge of her bed with her head in her hands. At two o'clock she stood at the window with the breeze fluttering her curtains, listening to an owl hooting close by. At three she lay in bed staring at the ceiling, wishing it was time for the sun to come up. She was just drifting off to sleep again when she felt it.

Like a breeze flitting across her cheek. Soft and light. Then a sound, a frantic light flapping sound.

Something brushed against her face. She felt the fleeting warmth of a small soft body, the flimsy paper-thin wings, the sharpness of claws – or was it fangs against her throat?

With a shriek she shot out of bed and flicked on the light. A bat was skimming around her room. It skittered and dive-bombed this way and that, seeking a way out.

Panic-stricken, Katie made a rush for the door but found it barricaded with the linen chest and chair. Gasping, keeping her head down, she clawed the furniture aside and shot out of the room, slamming the door on the creature.

For a second, she collapsed against the landing wall, trembling from head to toe. Just a bat, only a little bat, she told herself, trying to calm the furious pounding of her heart.

Bats were nothing to be afraid of. It must have flown into her room accidentally, through the open window. Poor thing, it would be more frightened than her.

She felt sick. Sick with terror, because she wasn't really thinking of harmless little pipistrelles. She was thinking of blood-sucking vampire bats.

Her hands went shakily to her throat for protection

as a chill crawled up her spine.

What was that flitting about her room? Just a harmless little bat that had lost its way?

Or a vampire bat—with a thirst for blood?

Her blood!

****

With a throw wrapped around her shoulders, Katie spent the rest of the night dozing fitfully downstairs on the sofa, trembling and jumping at the tiniest sound. She practically leapt out of her skin when the living room door opened.

Granddad looked equally as startled. "Katie! What are you doing up so early? Have you slept down here?"

She nodded bleakly, and he sat down beside her and wrapped his arms around her shoulders.

"You're still fretting about what you think you saw?" he said kindly. "I don't think there's anyone up in the attic. We'd have heard something by now."

"Why would we? That person, if it is a person, is hiding up there. You know it. You and Vanessa both know it!" Katie cried, her voice trembling. "Anyway, it's not just that. There was a bat in my bedroom this morning. It terrified me!"

"A bat?" he exclaimed, frowning. "No! That's impossible. It must have been a dream, all this talk of bats. No wonder it's upset you."

"Granddad, I didn't dream it. I was wide awake. It flitted all around my face. I felt it against my skin."

He raised his bushy eyebrows. "Well, I've never known bats to get into the house before, except in the attic. Let's go and see."

Still trembling, Katie followed him up the stairs, then stood well back while he went into her room.

"I can't see anything," he murmured, looking all around. He smiled kindly at her. "If it was here, it's gone now. It must have found its way back out through the window. It wouldn't have hurt you anyway, Katie."

"Really?" she queried. "Wouldn't that depend on whether it was a pipistrelle or a vampire bat, or even a vampire?"

"Katie!" he said gently, putting his arms around her again. "You're letting your imagination run away with you. If Vanessa's been frightening you with tales of vampires, that's just her sense of fun. You know what she's like. You used to love her scary stories."

"Yes…before. Not now that she's become so nasty and weird."

His shoulders slumped a little as he nodded his head sadly. "I know, I know. She's not the easiest person to live with these days." Rallying himself, he made a determined effort to look cheerful. "Anyway, today's her birthday. She's having a party and everything. I'm sure she'll be a different girl today. Come on, let's go down and have a nice early breakfast."

Katie had no desire to stay up here alone and so followed him back downstairs into the kitchen, where she helped him make scrambled eggs on toast.

"Actually, it's a big day for me too," he said, moving quite sprightly around the kitchen. "It's the election of the town mayor tonight, and I've a feeling that it might actually fall on my shoulders this year."

He looked so happy, Katie managed a smile. "I hope they do choose you, Granddad. That would be fantastic."

She turned away, in case he read her thoughts. She probably wouldn't find out if he was elected or not, as she would be long gone by the time he got back from his meeting.

It was a shame; the excitement of being elected, if he was chosen, would be spoilt when he discovered she'd gone.

She was relieved that he hadn't spotted her packed suitcase or noticed the absence of clothes in her wardrobe when he'd gone looking for the bat. She didn't want to have to explain. All she knew was that she couldn't stay here any longer. There was something in the attic. He and Vanessa were covering up, lying to her.

Breakfast that morning was the first and only meal she'd actually enjoyed since arriving here. For once there wasn't the usual unpleasant atmosphere that

Vanessa seemed to spread wherever she went. It was just her and Granddad, chatting about normal things. He wanted to know about her school and her interests and her mum.

By the time they'd washed up the breakfast plates and he was preparing to get some work done in his study before setting off to a whole round of meetings, Katie impulsively kissed his cheek.

"What was that for?" he asked, his face lighting up.

"For luck," she said simply. He would need it, living here with Vanessa.

It was also a kiss goodbye.

Katie's plan was to walk to the railway station and get the times for the trains home. Then she would come back to the bakehouse, pick up her suitcase, and leave without anyone noticing.

With Granddad back in his study, Katie went up to her room, half expecting the bat to swoop out of some dark corner at her, or something far worse. She pushed the door open and stood for a moment not venturing in. Then she stepped forward, looking all around.

Glancing upwards, she had the urge to shout, "I know you're there, Christian!"

Only she wasn't that sure it was Christian and not some ancient vampire that had crawled out of its grave, thirsty for blood.

She finished her final bits of packing, feeling guilty about taking her nanna's possessions, but if it was what

111

Granddad wanted, then she couldn't refuse.

As she busied herself, she listened for sounds from above. She heard nothing.

And then she remembered.

Vampires slept during the day, didn't they?

****

Walking down the lane towards the village, Katie found herself peering through the trees, not quite sure whether it was in case anything nasty was lurking in the woods, or whether she was vaguely hoping to bump into Vanessa's blue-eyed friend again.

Deep down, she really wanted to see Christian, to prove to herself that she was being stupid in thinking he was some horrific blood-sucking creature of the night. Only why was he never around in the daytime? She'd only ever seen him at twilight, when the bats come out, or in the shade, like an overhanging tree, or in a crypt in the graveyard when the sky was black.

She was shivering by the time she reached the village, even though the day was bright and sunny.

The railway station was another long walk; her legs ached, and the lack of sleep had left her feeling quite weary by the time she reached it. Finding the ticket office, she enquired about the next train home.

"Sorry, m'dear," the man behind the counter said. "There's no trains running at all from this station until

Monday. They're doing track repairs."

Katie gripped the edge of the counter, feeling her legs give way. "There has to be! I have to get home today. Aren't there any coaches?"

He checked his computer, running his finger down a list of numbers and names on his screen. "Nothing direct from here. You'd have to get the bus from here to Wincaster, that's a twenty-minute ride; then catch the coach from there."

"That's fine. I'll do that then. What time is the next coach from there?"

He checked the big clock on the wall. "Four minutes ago. Then ten o' clock tomorrow morning."

She felt numb. "So, I've missed today's coach?"

"I'm afraid so. Hey, don't look so downcast. What you need to do tomorrow is be here at nine twenty for the bus. That'll get you to Wincaster in time for the coach."

"Thank you." She turned and walked away, in a daze, walking blindly, not looking where she was going. Not caring. All she was aware of was that she couldn't escape today. She was stuck here for Vanessa's party, which wouldn't please her. And worse, she would be spending another night under the same roof as that *thing*.

The day felt endless. Katie walked the streets until her legs ached. She read an entire book in the library, staying there so long the librarian asked her if she was all right. She ate in a little café, sitting alone, watching passers-by through the window. The only bright spot of the day was phoning the hospital and speaking to her mum.

She sounded bright and said the doctors were delighted with the outcome of her operation. They'd removed the tumour successfully and she'd be back home by the end of the week.

Katie had squeezed her eyes shut as she clung onto the phone. Desperately she held back the tears of relief. She didn't tell her mum that she might actually see her sooner than she thought.

If she managed to get the coach home, she'd be back by this time tomorrow. Vanessa and the bats would be well behind her.

But poor Granddad, stuck here, with Vanessa goading him, bringing on his angina attacks, not caring.

And what would happen next time he had a bad attack and couldn't get at his pills quickly enough?

Katie knew only too well...

****

By seven o'clock that evening, the last thing Katie felt like doing was sitting through a talk on bats. If she never saw another bat again in her life, she would be happy. But with nothing else to do, and no desire at all to go back to the bakehouse and intrude on Vanessa's party, she pushed open the swinging doors of the village hall. She was faced with regimented rows of hard-backed chairs and the smell of floor polish invaded her senses.

There were about twenty people, who, apparently like her, had nothing better to do on a Saturday evening. But most of them seemed to know each other and chatted amongst themselves as they waited for the speaker to get his notes and slide show in order.

The talk began, with photographs flashed up on a large screen. Katie shuddered as huge images of bats hovered on the wall.

Their sharp little faces looked evil to her now. Those harmless fruit-eating bats didn't look harmless to her. They all looked as if they could grow fangs and bite through the tough skin of a cow, or anything else for that matter.

At the end of the talk, the speaker asked if there were any questions. Half a dozen hands went up, and he worked through their questions in turn, displaying an impressive knowledge about the subject.

Finally, Katie put her hand up.

"Yes, young lady?"

Her cheeks turned pink as everyone turned to stare at her.

She cleared her throat. "Do you believe in vampires?"

A little ripple of laughter went around the room.

The speaker smiled.

"Vampire bats, I assume you're referring to, and yes, certain species…"

"No! Actual vampires! People! The sort that drink blood, like we see in movies." She felt everyone's eyes on her. They probably thought she was being ridiculous, but she kept on. "Like the boy who was supposed to be entombed alive in the seventeenth century, right here in the local cemetery? Do you believe it's possible that he's got out, and he's right here, back in the village?"

More laughter, but Katie remained waiting for his answer, aware that people now were whispering about her.

The speaker realised she was serious and wiped the smile off his face. "It's an excellent question. I wasn't aware of this legend. I don't actually come from around here, but I'd say the answer is no, there's no such thing as those kind of vampires. At least I hope not."

He allowed himself another smile and a look around his audience for approval.

A woman in a flowery dress half turned in her seat. "Actually, I can understand why she's asking, there's been rumours of someone looking very vampirish hanging around Oatmeal Woods. I did actually mention it to my husband. He's a policeman. He said he'd check it out."

Another ripple of conversations ran through the

audience, and the speaker, sensing he was losing his audience, rounded the evening up and took his applause with a little bow.

Katie left.

Chapter Ten

Returning to the old bakehouse past the woods was a nightmare. It was twilight and she shuddered as she hurried past the shadowed trees. She didn't want to go back to the house yet, but if she stayed out any longer, it would be pitch black and the walk would be too eerie.

Vanessa's party would no doubt be in full swing, but there was nothing she could do about that. She'd just go straight up to her room and keep out of everyone's way. She couldn't stay out all night.

Especially with a vampire on the loose.

She told herself to stop being stupid. It had probably been Vanessa climbing the wall last night—another one of her spiteful tricks to scare her.

As the bakehouse loomed into view, Katie felt a twinge of unease.

The house was in darkness.

Her step faltered. She'd expected a blaze of lights and music booming from the rafters. Not silence, not darkness.

She felt suddenly jittery, her skin prickling as she stepped up to the front door. With the key clutched in her hand, she stopped and listened.

Not a sound.

Not a glass clinking, not a voice, not a whisper of music...nothing.

She moved back from the door and stared up at the old house. All the curtains were drawn shut. She crept around to the front window and tried to peer through a gap in the curtains. She thought she could see a glimmer of red, but it was a strange, dim red glow, flickering.

She went back to the door and turned the key — and hesitated. The feeling of dread sending shivers down her spine.

Something wasn't right.

Nervously, she let herself in. Then she heard the music. The heavy oak door and thick walls had made the house almost soundproof. But now she could hear it — just.

It was soft choir music, not the sort of music for a party. A classical piece. She'd heard it before and never liked it. It had been used throughout a horror film which she had watched once, at Vanessa's suggestion. The film had terrified her, and whenever she heard this particular piece, it brought back all the terrors of the film.

It was playing softly, and Katie couldn't quite figure out where it was coming from. It seemed to be all around her, like evil whisperings coming from every corner or every room.

The hall was in pitch darkness, and she felt for the light switch and clicked it down. Nothing happened. Frantically she tried it a few more times. Still nothing.

A power failure? It couldn't be if there was music

playing.

She found her way through to the kitchen and tried the lights there. Again nothing.

A fuse must have blown.

Stubbing her toe against the table, she turned and fumbled her way to the sitting room where she thought she'd glimpsed a dim flickering red glow.

She pushed open the door and gasped.

The room was bathed in candlelight. Thick, tall candles stood in holders all around the room, filling it with quivering shadows.

The room had been decked out for a party. Balloons and streamers hung from walls and ceilings, fluttering gently as she stirred the air with her presence.

Katie stood in the centre of the deserted room. She had to conclude that Vanessa had done herself proud in preparing the setting for her birthday party – her surprise birthday party.

Wait and see what the surprise is…

She had created a colour theme for the event.

Black!

Black balloons, black streamers. As black as the heart of the girl who had set this all up.

Poor, poor Granddad. He was going to walk in on this.

She heard a footfall on the stairs, and afraid of what was coming next, Katie ducked down behind the sofa, crouching into a tight ball, keeping out of sight.

She could smell the heady perfume that Vanessa wore, filling the room, and peeping out from around the side of the sofa, she glimpsed Vanessa's feet in open-toed sandals, and a long floating dress made of black chiffon.

As Vanessa moved softly and silently around the room, Katie caught a full glimpse of her black-hearted cousin.

Her make-up was perfection, black rimmed eyes against a pure white face. Lips painted a dark blood red. Hair, drifting loose around her slender shoulders. She looked stunning, and terrifying.

A moment later, they both heard the key turning in the front door.

Granddad was home.

His voice rang out. "Wonderful news! They've made me Lord Mayor!"

And then fell silent.

Katie heard him futilely clicking the light switch in the hall. "Vanessa! Vanessa, are you here? What's happened to the electrics?" And then he walked into the living room and gasped.

"Hello, Granddad!" Vanessa greeted him. "Welcome to my surprise party."

"What's happened to the lights?" he asked, standing in the doorway.

"We have candles," breathed Vanessa. "Aren't they pretty?"

"But where are your friends? Are they late?"

"Friends?" Vanessa murmured, gliding right past Katie as she remained hiding. "I have no friends, Granddad. You saw to that, didn't you, when you killed Michael."

Katie almost cried out. Granddad had killed someone!

Somehow, she managed to stay quiet as the reason for Vanessa's blackmail became clear.

Granddad had killed Vanessa's friend!

"I didn't mean it to happen," Granddad cried, sounding angry. "You know that was the last thing I'd ever want to do. It was an accident."

"Some accident," Vanessa retaliated. "You find us having a nice time, chatting up there in the attic, doing no harm, and you start ranting and raving about having a boy upstairs. Nanna knew we were there. She knew we weren't doing anything wrong. But you flew into a rage, didn't you? Dragging me out of the attic, slamming the door on him. Do you remember what you shouted?"

"Yes, please don't, Vanessa," Granddad uttered, sounding defeated.

But she wasn't about to stop now. "You yelled: 'You want to be there, then stay there. Stay there and rot!' Remember, Granddad, remember?"

"I didn't mean it…"

"And then, poor Nanna tried to calm you down and

you pushed her aside. You wouldn't listen to anyone. Poor Nanna…" Vanessa's voice broke into a sob. "Nanna had her attack, and she died…"

"I didn't mean to," Granddad said wretchedly. Katie closed her eyes, picturing the awful scene.

"No, I know you didn't mean for Nanna to die. I'm not stupid," snapped Vanessa. "But you didn't give Michael a second thought, did you?"

"I forgot he was locked in," Granddad said. "What with your nanna collapsing, and the doctor coming and her passing away and then the funeral…"

"Weeks flew by," Vanessa butted in. "How long was it until I reminded you that you'd locked Michael in the attic – a month?"

"Why didn't you remind me sooner?" he tried to argue.

From her hiding place Katie wondered the same thing, but Vanessa was in no mood to explain herself and snapped back at him.

"Don't blame me. You're the one who locked him in and told him to rot. You're the one who couldn't even bear to look when I did tell you. What did you do? You bricked up the doorway and sealed his body in forever."

"I'm sorry…I'm sorry, Vanessa, you know how sorry I am."

Katie glimpsed her granddad going imploringly towards her, but Vanessa backed away.

123

"If he hadn't been in care; if he hadn't run off from foster families before, the police would have come looking here for him. But nobody really cared about Michael, only me."

"Please...won't you ever forgive me?"

"No! Why should I?" Vanessa cried. "You told him to rot, and he did rot. His skin rotted, his lovely blond hair rotted, his clothing rotted away to rags. But do you know what, Granddad? He doesn't bear a grudge. In fact, he wants to come and say hello again to you."

"What?" Granddad gasped, his voice more a croak than a word, and Katie saw him grab hold of the sideboard for support.

Vanessa's black-rimmed eyes became huge. "Yes, Michael is our surprise guest. Michael! Michael, please come down and join the party."

For a few seconds there was silence. No one even seemed to breathe. And then came the heavy thud of someone's foot on the top stair.

Then another...*thud!*

"Vanessa..." Granddad cried, his voice shaking with fear. "It's not...It can't be..."

Thud....thud! Slow pained footsteps, as if every movement was a monumental effort.

Barely aware of her movements, Katie came out from her hiding place. She could see into the hallway from here but neither Vanessa nor Granddad were aware of her standing there. All eyes were fixed on the figure coming slowly down the stairs.

Both Katie and Granddad cried out in terror as they saw him.

He was tall…or rather he would have been tall. Now he was stooped and broken like an old man; his jeans and T-shirt were filthy and in tatters; his hair, which must have been blond at one time was grey and hung in rats' tails around a face that was green and grey, with skin dangling off in ugly clumps.

Wait and see what the surprise is!

He reached the bottom stair and turned, zombie-like, towards the living room. Granddad backed off, clutching at his chest. Katie ran to him, petrified of the monstrosity that had joined them.

Vanessa saw her then and screeched at her. "You!" But Granddad could only stare at the ghoul…Michael.

Katie clung onto her granddad, barely able to believe her eyes. This was what lived in the attic. This half dead creature. How then did he scale the outside wall so nimbly?

Reality dawned so swiftly, it was like someone had thrown an icy bucket of water over her.

It was someone in disguise.

She looked intently at the horrific face and saw, beyond the ghoulish paint and make-up, the most incredibly ocean-blue eyes looking out.

The boy she'd seen in the village. The one who reads adventure novels from the library. No wonder he had so many, the hours and days he must have spent living up there in the attic.

And no wonder they hadn't wanted Christian to look into the attic that day when he'd gone up the ladder.

Granddad thought he'd see the dead body of a boy. While Vanessa knew he'd find a gorgeous blue-eyed, blond boyfriend who'd probably made a home for himself up there. No wonder Vanessa let Granddad believe he'd actually locked the boy in. It was understandable that he'd forgotten. And Vanessa had spitefully turned the situation around to get the upper hand on him. To blackmail him. And the poor man had fallen for it.

No doubt there was a trapdoor in Vanessa's room, allowing her access to feed him. Perhaps inside one of her built-in cupboards.

"He's in disguise, Granddad!" Katie exclaimed. "Granddad, look at him. He's wearing make-up." And to prove it, she wiped her hand angrily down the boy's face and showed her paint-smeared fingers to her granddad. "Look! It's make-up!"

But it was too late. Granddad's heart had already started to fail him. His lips were tinged with blue.

"Granddad, no…Where's your pills?" She found them in his pocket and unscrewed the lid, her own hands shaking violently.

The pill box was empty.

"Granddad, your pills, where are they?"

He looked distraught. "Should be there…I don't understand."

Katie turned to her cousin and saw the look of triumph in her eyes as their granddad slid to the floor. "You took them!"

But Vanessa's eyes simply widened. "Go on, Michael, you haven't shaken Granddad's hand yet. Show him there are no hard feelings."

"Stop it!" Katie cried, standing between the monster and her granddad, even though the boy had made no move to reach out his hand and do as Vanessa ordered. In fact, he shook his head and backed away.

He spoke then, and Katie recognised his voice, knowing for sure that he was the boy she'd met the other day. "Enough, Vanessa! Your granddad looks really ill. Hey, I only wanted to give him a scare. I don't want to kill the old boy."

"Shut up!" Vanessa screamed at him. "You idiot. He knows now, he knows!"

"Yes he does. So you won't be able to blackmail him over this anymore!" Katie cried, racing into his study and scrambling about on the floor in the darkness to try and find one of the pills that went scattering the other day. To her relief she found one and raced back into the other room.

Michael was holding Granddad in his arms, murmuring how sorry he was.

127

Katie slipped the pill under her granddad's tongue, and his eyelids fluttered.

"Vanessa... how you must hate me," the old man murmured.

Vanessa had been standing a little aside, watching as Katie and Michael frantically tried to save his life. Glancing her way, Katie had thought her cousin didn't care. She seemed to have detached herself from the scene. But hearing a sudden sob as Katie knelt beside her granddad, she looked up to see tears streaming down Vanessa's cheeks.

Then Vanessa crumpled to her knees and clutched her granddad's hand, bringing it to her lips. "I blamed you for Nanna dying. You know that, don't you?"

He managed to nod his head. In barely a whisper he said, "I shouldn't have shouted and raged. It was unforgivable."

"I wanted to punish you," Vanessa sobbed. "I hated you. I wanted revenge for Nanna dying."

Michael spoke then, but his voice cracked, as he tried to hold back the tears. "Well, you've certainly got revenge all right!"

"I'm sorry!" Vanessa uttered. "But I don't want you to die. I thought I did. I emptied your pill box. I wanted to scare you to death..." She began to sob hysterically. "Don't die, Granddad, please don't die. I need you!"

"She's heart-broken over her Nan," Michael said to Katie. "I didn't know all this stuff was going on in her head. She didn't tell me. I thought it was just a prank."

The old man's eye's crinkled, and he squeezed Vanessa's hands. "Forgive me…"

His eyes closed. His head slumped.

Vanessa gave an agonised sob and fled. Throwing wide the front door, she ran distraught out into the night.

Michael felt for Granddad's pulse, while Katie rubbed her granddad's hands and chest, not knowing what else to do.

"He's got a pulse," Michael said. "It's pretty strong, and his heartbeat feels regular. I think he just passed out. I'm going to call for an ambulance. I'll catch up with Vanessa too. Stay here. He'll be all right, honestly."

As Michael went racing out of the house, probably all set to give any passers-by the fright of their lives, Katie concentrated on bringing her grandfather around.

****

He would have to be careful. People were alerted to his presence. Already the police were seeking him out. If they caught him, he had no doubt that they would seal him into a crypt like before. A crypt that had taken him almost three hundred years to claw his way out of.

Or worse, maybe people now knew that a wooden stake through the heart was how to kill a vampire.

Yes, he would have to be very careful.

But what was this...? A girl dressed in a floating black dress, racing like the wind towards him.

He knew her instantly, it was Katie's crazy cousin.

Running his tongue over the tips of his fangs, William Knight, or Christian as he was known to his acquaintances, crouched amongst the low branches of the trees to wait until she came close enough.

And then it would be a pleasure...

Chapter Eleven

Katie had taken a taxi back from the hospital, leaving her granddad in safe hands. He was fully conscious and making a good recovery. But the hospital staff as well as Katie and her granddad had been surprised when Vanessa and Michael had walked hand-in-hand into the ward. Michael had washed off most of his make-up, but still raised a few eyebrows amongst the other patients and nurses.

When Vanessa had seen her granddad sitting up in bed, her face had crumpled and she'd run to him. She couldn't speak, tears of relief were flooding from her eyes. So she had simply hugged him. And he had hugged her back.

He held no grudge, and by the time the nurse instructed them all to go home so Granddad could rest, the only tears being shed were ones of happiness.

Vanessa made Michael up a bed in a spare bedroom, and he joked about missing his makeshift bed in the attic.

Katie left them to it and fell into her own bed, exhausted. It wasn't long before she heard a tap on the door, however. Vanessa opened it and poked her head around. "May I come in?"

"Yes!" Katie exclaimed, delighted to have her cousin back.

She edged over to allow Vanessa to sit beside her.

"I thought you'd hate me," Vanessa said, tucking her legs beneath her. "You'd have every right."

"I'm not one to bear a grudge. I'm just glad we're friends again," Katie answered, smiling.

"Thank goodness for that," said Vanessa. "But I am sorry I was so awful to you."

"You were! But great tricks! The way you flitted around like a vampire in the cow field. And that giant bat you rigged up in the barn was amazing."

"I didn't do those things, Katie," Vanessa said softly. "I wasn't going to tell you. I didn't want to frighten you anymore. But that wasn't me."

A delicious tingle ran down Katie's spine, recognising her cousin's art for a good humoured scary story. She suddenly knew she was in for one. "Go on."

"It wasn't me! Honestly! We have actually had a visit from the vampire that was in the crypt. I told you last Halloween he broke out, didn't I?"

"You mean vandals broke in," Katie corrected her.
"Believe what you like," Vanessa said lightly. "But he actually did. And you'll never guess who he actually was."

"Go on, surprise me."

"Bat Boy. Your pal Christian."

Katie laughed. "Nice one, Vanessa."

"I'm serious. I saw him. Earlier tonight, when I went running down the lane, you know, after what happened to Granddad."

"Yes," Katie said warily.

"Christian was there, hiding amongst the trees in Oatmeal Woods."

Katie chuckled. This was definitely like old times – Vanessa and her stories. Hugging herself, she settled down to listen. "Go on. What happened?"

"Well, I was running down the lane when suddenly this figure in a black cloak leapt out in front of me. It was Christian, looking like a young Dracula, I swear. He had slicked black hair that went into a point down his forehead, swarthy olive skin, and two white fangs. I screamed and dodged behind a tree, but he came at me, saying he wanted to drink my blood."

"Go on," Katie said, unable to stop herself from grinning. "Well, I wasn't having that, so I just sort of pulled a tree branch back and let it go. It catapulted right into him, and well, it must have had a sharp wooden branch sticking out, because it speared him right through the heart and he vanished into a cloud of dust."

Katie laughed and clapped her hands. "Oh, Vanessa, you don't know how great it is to hear your spooky stories again."

Vanessa looked shocked. "I'm not story-telling. It's the truth."

"Yeah, yeah!"

"You don't believe me? Okay, then I'll tell you what

actually happened, shall I?" She softened her voice, so it became a whisper, and lowered her head so her hair curtained her pale face. Her eyes glittered.

"He came from nowhere... Suddenly he was standing before me. I knew straightaway it was Christian. Only he was taller, broader, with a sweeping cloak that billowed in the night. His mouth opened, and it was like a glimpse into an abyss, and before I could run, he swooped down onto my throat. I felt my own warm blood trickling down my skin and as he drew back, it was dripping from his fangs. Then in a second, he swirled his cloak around him and transformed himself into a bat. In the blink of an eye, he was gone."

"Fantastic!" laughed Katie. "Excellent! So that makes you a vampire too now."

Vanessa's voice was still soft. "So, you still don't believe me. Then I'll prove it to you..."

Katie's laughter died as Vanessa moved closer. Her skin began to prickle as slowly, very slowly Vanessa lifted up her long black hair and turned her head to one side to show Katie her pale white throat, and as she did, her blood-red lips parted.

Katie had never noticed how sharp and pointed her cousin's white incisors were, until now...

Ends

About the Author

Ann Evans is an English writer with around 40 books to her name. She writes for children, young adults, reluctant readers, adults and non-fiction. She was a feature writer for her local newspaper the *Coventry Telegraph* for 13 years, which was where the idea for this book was sparked. She regularly writes magazine articles on all kinds of topics from animals to antiques. She also runs writing workshops for adults and does author visits in schools.

Ann began writing as a hobby when her three children were little. They are all grown up now with children of their own. That hobby seemed to take over, becoming a full-time career.

Discover more of Ann Evans' books on her website and keep in touch on Social Media:
www.annevansbooks.co.uk
https://www.facebook.com/annevansbooks/
https://twitter.com/annevansauthor

A note from the author:

Thank you for buying this book, I really hope you've enjoyed it. If you have, perhaps you would consider leaving a review on Amazon or Goodreads.

Thank you.

Ann Evans

Have you read these KS2/YA books by Ann Evans?

Celeste
The Beast
The Reawakening
Rampage
Cry Danger
Deadly Hunter
The Trunk
Fishing for Clues
Stealing the Show
Pushing his Luck
Pointing the Finger

Short reads for reluctant readers:
Nightmare
Red Handed
Straw Men
Kicked into Touch
How to Spend Like a Celebrity
By My Side
Blank
Living the Lie
Keeper
Runaway
Promise Me
A Little Secret
The Prize
Message Alert
Viral

Printed in Great Britain
by Amazon